# Cinderellas in the Spotlight

*Could their Prince Charmings be waiting under the mistletoe?*

It all started so innocently at a TV studio...but what happens next will become the start of a Christmas neither Celeste nor her best friend, Rachel, will ever forget!

Because when Rachel is asked to make up the numbers for the filming of a New Year's Eve party, a pretend midnight kiss with Celeste's delectable brother, Damon, feels anything but fake!

While next door, when Celeste clashes with TV quiz host Theo, she can't help but wonder if the sparks flying between them could mean something more than television banter...

What's clear is now is the time for these two heroines to stand in the spotlight while they discover they are worthy of meeting their perfect princes!

*Awakening His Shy Cinderella*
available in December

This Christmas, a shy, awkward Cinderella finally learns to ask for what she really wants: love...with her best friend's younger brother!

*A Midnight Kiss to Seal the Deal*
available in January

Can a pretend Christmas romance between two complete opposites lead to true love by the time Big Ben strikes midnight on New Year's Eve?

Dear Reader,

I wrote and edited *Awakening His Shy Cinderella* in lockdown, during the 2020 global pandemic. I was writing about a city that no longer existed—not in that moment, and not even now. A bustling, busy city full of activity and people and hugs and crowds. I don't know yet what the world will look like when you read this, but I hope we're on our way back to something more familiar.

Whatever the circumstances under which you're reading Rachel and Damon's story, I hope it gives you hope. Hope for our world, and hope for yourself. Because I think Christmas is a time for hope—and love, and joy, and kindness. So those are the feelings I poured into this book as I wrote, as my Christmas present to you.

With love, and hope, this Christmastime,

*Sophie* x

# Awakening His Shy Cinderella

**Sophie Pembroke**

## HARLEQUIN®
### Romance™

Recycling programs
for this product may
not exist in your area.

ISBN-13: 978-1-335-55655-4

Awakening His Shy Cinderella

Copyright © 2020 by Sophie Pembroke

This edition published by arrangement with Harlequin Books S.A.

For questions and comments about the quality of this book,
please contact us at CustomerService@Harlequin.com.

Harlequin Enterprises ULC
22 Adelaide St. West, 40th Floor
Toronto, Ontario M5H 4E3, Canada
www.Harlequin.com

Printed in U.S.A.

**Sophie Pembroke** has been dreaming, reading and writing romance ever since she read her first Harlequin as part of her English literature degree at Lancaster University, so getting to write romance fiction for a living really is a dream come true! Born in Abu Dhabi, Sophie grew up in Wales and now lives in a little Hertfordshire market town with her scientist husband, her incredibly imaginative and creative daughter, and her adventurous, adorable little boy. In Sophie's world, happy *is* forever after, everything stops for tea and there's always time for one more page...

### Books by Sophie Pembroke

### Harlequin Romance

#### *A Fairytale Summer!*
*Italian Escape with Her Fake Fiancé*

#### *The Cattaneos' Christmas Miracles*
*CEO's Marriage Miracle*

#### *Wedding Island*
*Island Fling to Forever*

*Road Trip with the Best Man*
*Carrying Her Millionaire's Baby*
*Pregnant on the Earl's Doorstep*
*Snowbound with the Heir*
*Second Chance for the Single Mom*

Visit the Author Profile page at Harlequin.com for more titles.

For London, my favourite city in the world—
especially at Christmastime.

# CHAPTER ONE

RACHEL CHARLES HELD the skimpy piece of sequinned fabric against her body, sighing at her reflection in the changing-room mirror. If it even stretched across her curves, she imagined she'd look alarmingly like a disco ball, in both shape and blinding capability. Not exactly the look she wanted to project at the Hartbury & Sons department store Christmas party—especially not as the stepdaughter of the last remaining Hartbury in the business.

There were no '& Sons' any more—just Rachel's stepmother, Hannah, and her two stepsisters, Gretchen and Maisie. And Rachel's father, of course, since he'd married Hannah and become an enthusiastic part of the Hartbury family.

Unlike her.

She tossed the disco-ball dress in the direction of the pile building up on the chair in the corner of the large changing area. The store was closing, so she didn't need to worry about any customers coming in.

That didn't mean she was without an audience, though.

'What was wrong with that one?' Maisie asked, from her relaxed position draped across the chaise longue beside the full-length mirror. 'I thought it was perfectly festive.'

This was the problem with sisters—something Rachel hadn't experienced until she was in her early teens and her father remarried. For some reason, they seemed invested in Rachel's wardrobe—although in this case she suspected it was so Maisie could borrow the dress once Rachel inevitably chickened out of wearing it to the party after she'd bought it.

'I think that one's maybe more your style, Maisie,' she said dryly, reaching for the next contender in the pile. 'You'd look fantastic in it.'

How had her stepsisters even got involved in this shopping expedition anyway? Rachel had casually mentioned, when asked by her stepmother if she'd decided what she was wearing to the party, that she'd probably just wear the same black dress as last year. And then, the minute she finished her shift on the till that evening, Gretchen and Maisie had been there waiting, their arms full of half the stock from the womenswear floor, their smiles beaming enthusiasm at her.

She wanted to believe that it was a sweet, sisterly gesture. Maybe before last summer she'd have even been able to convince herself of that. But not now.

Now, she knew as fact, rather than just suspicion, what her stepsisters really thought of her—thanks to Tobias. At least she had something to thank her sort-of ex for, she supposed.

*Just a few more weeks*, Rachel reminded herself, as she drew the curtain on the changing room. As soon as her father's next set of test results came in, and he had his meeting with the consultant, she'd be ready to act. To move on and move out, at last, from the Hartbury family home.

It had made sense after university to move back home for a while. After all, Hartbury House was a four-storey town house in central London. It had plenty of room for the five of them and was far better positioned than anything she could have afforded on her own—even when she finally managed to get a job.

That had been the next issue, of course—finding employment. Her Oxford degree went a long way on application forms, but her lack of confidence made interviews a nightmare. Many Oxford grads she knew had come out of university with a determination to embrace opportunity, believing they could do anything.

Somehow, she'd emerged with the opposite world view. And apparently it showed in job interviews.

So when Hannah had suggested she work at the family business for a while, just until she found her feet, it had seemed like a logical next step. She'd found her own niche there, beyond just working on the shop floor, and had started to feel as if she might even be making a difference. Seven years later, it was hard to imagine working anywhere else.

She shook her head to stop her wool-gathering, and wriggled into the next dress on the pile. One thing at a time, that was how she had to do this.

First, she needed to know that her father was really okay after that terrifying rush into hospital earlier in the year, him clutching at his chest, and her trying to remember all the details of his blood-pressure medication to tell the doctors. She wouldn't get that assurance until nearer Christmas, maybe even the new year. That was the time to think about using her hoarded savings to find her own place to live. Then, once she was settled, she could think about maybe changing jobs.

One step at a time. Starting with finding a dress for the Christmas party.

The next dress was plain, a green velvet thing that stretched from her chin to her ankles, stopping at her wrists on the way. She supposed it was a little bit better than the disco ball—until Gretchen handed her a pom-pom-laden wrap to wear over it. 'To, you know, hide your lumpy bits.'

Rachel winced at her reflection. *I look like a Christmas tree.* But she'd promised to try to keep the peace with her stepsisters, for her father's sake. He'd been so upset by their row last summer, after everything went down with Tobias, and Hannah believed that stress must have added to his heart problems. Maybe even caused the heart attack that followed not so long after.

Rachel was less convinced, but she wasn't going to risk it. However much Gretchen and Maisie provoked her.

*Two months at the most, and I'll be out of here. I hope.*

'It's very…festive,' she said.

Gretchen beamed. 'Exactly! And I knew you wouldn't want to feel uncomfortable and on display,' she added, shooting a look at the disco-ball dress, which had somehow made its way into Maisie's grasp.

*She's trying to be kind. She knows I'm self-conscious about my curves.* Maybe if she repeated the words enough inside her head it would be easier to believe them.

This was the *other* problem with sisters—well, with having two gorgeous, willowy stepsisters with legs that went on for ever and which often featured in the celebrity gossip pages, demurely climbing out of cars arriving at the latest hot spot or party. Gretchen and Maisie were heiresses in their own right, courtesy of their late, great father, the famed tycoon Howard Jacobs. Their money, combined with their looks, made them It Girls, the ones to be seen with around London.

Rachel was none of those things. Not tall or willowy, not rich or beautiful. She was short, curvy, and while she liked to think her face wasn't actively offensive, it was really quite normal, under her cloud of curly brown hair.

Gretchen and Maisie obviously found her a sartorial puzzle to solve. Maisie tried to put her in the sort of things she would wear, and Gretchen tried to disguise all her disagreeable parts.

Rachel sighed and thought wistfully of her old black dress at home.

Out of the entire pile of dresses her stepsisters had shown up with, there had only been one she'd liked—and that, Gretchen admitted, she'd only picked up by mistake. It was cranberry red with navy stags, owls and a woodland print across it, knee length, with a wrap front top and, best of all, pockets. Gretchen had whipped it away as soon as she'd selected it, though, declaring that it would draw far too much attention to her curves. Even Maisie had nodded, adding that it didn't even have any sparkle to distract the eye.

Because apparently she was so disgusting to look at that people's eyes needed to be distracted.

She studied the Christmas tree outfit again. Maybe if she took off the pom-pom wrap…

'Well, that's a look.'

Rachel froze. She knew that voice. That low, warm voice with humour lurking behind it. There was no cruelty in it, but that didn't stop her insides curling up and dying from embarrassment.

Damon Hunter. Her best friend's younger brother, the most attractive man she'd ever met in real life and, incidentally, the last person on the planet she wanted to see her dressed up like a Christmas tree.

Well, this was just *ideal*.

Forcing herself to take a deep breath, she looked up from studying the pom-poms on the wrap, and met his gaze in the mirror. 'Hello, Damon. What are you doing here?'

Her voice was even, friendly, and she was proud of herself for managing that much. She might look like a Christmas tree, but that didn't mean she had to throw all dignity to the winds.

She'd been hiding her crush on Celeste's little brother for the best part of a decade. It was second nature at this point.

'Celeste sent me to pick you up. For some reason she seemed to think you'd try and wriggle out of attending this thing tonight.'

That was because Celeste knew her too well. From the moment they'd been put together in the halls of residence at university, along with three boys whose only interests were rugby, beer and pulling unsuspecting girls in freshers' week, Rachel and Celeste had been best mates. Rachel had always suspected that, if it hadn't been for those circumstances, the two of them would probably never even have met, let alone become friends. Neither of them was exactly the outgoing, friend-making type. In fact, she suspected she might be Celeste's *only* friend, the only person she'd ever looked up from her studies long enough to get to know.

It might have been sheer convenience, but Rachel still felt a little special, knowing that.

'You're going out tonight?' Gretchen asked, sounding faintly astonished. Rachel didn't take it personally; she was pretty surprised too.

'Where are you going?' Maisie had straightened a little on the chaise longue, her endless legs folded in the way that showed them off best, angled towards Damon, of course. 'Can we come? Unless it's a hot date, of course…' She and Gretchen couldn't help but giggle at that idea, apparently. Again, Rachel couldn't bring herself to blame them for it. The idea of gorgeous, outgoing, charming and successful Damon Hunter going on a date with a shy and dumpy shop girl *was* pretty hilarious.

Sighing, Rachel turned at last and faced Damon's amused gaze in reality, rather than just reflection. 'Damon, these are my stepsisters, Gretchen and Maisie. And this is Damon, Celeste's brother.' The girls looked blank at the mention of Celeste. 'My best friend, Celeste,' Rachel clarified.

'Oh, right!' Gretchen clapped her hands together as she placed the name, then turned to Damon with a conspiratorial smile. 'To be honest, we kind of thought Rachel had invented Celeste for the longest time. It's not like we ever see her.'

'Although if we'd known she had a brother that looked like you—' Maisie muttered, until Gretchen shot her a warning look.

'My sister isn't the most sociable of people,' Damon said, with an easy smile.

'Understatement,' Rachel mumbled. Damon obviously heard it though, as he shot her an amused look. Turning her head to hide her blush, she ducked into the changing cubicle again, drawing the curtain tight closed as she changed back into normal, non-Christmas-tree clothes. The curtain, and the rustle of velvet, did nothing to cover the sound of her stepsisters flirting with Damon, though.

She forced herself to think positively about it. Gretchen and Maisie were *exactly* the sort of women Damon dated—usually for about a fortnight, before moving on. Maybe if one or both of them were distracted by Damon for a while, they'd stop their latest humiliation tactic of dressing her up in Christmas ornaments. That was a bonus, right?

And really, she'd spent nearly ten years watching Damon date other women—starting with the fresher girl he pulled in that nightclub when he came to stay with her and Celeste in their second year of university. It wasn't as if he was ever going to date *her*, so what difference did it make *who* he dated?

It did, of course. But she swallowed the thought and pulled her black and grey jumper dress over her head instead.

'My sister is taking part in some weirdly academic quiz show about Christmas tonight,' Damon was saying when she emerged from the thick woollen cocoon. 'She wants Rachel and me in the audience to cheer her on.'

Gretchen and Maisie's enthusiasm about joining them for the evening obviously waned when they heard their plans. But as Rachel emerged from the changing room, Maisie was listing places in London Damon should try for the nightlife—*and maybe he would see her there.*

'Ready?' Damon asked, the minute Rachel emerged.

Rachel nodded, but before she could grab her bag her stepmother, Hannah, appeared looking flustered.

'*There* you are!' She reached out to grab Rachel's arm. 'There's been an absolute disaster with one of the window displays. Some brat climbed in to try and get one of those silly mice you've put in every one of them and knocked half of it over. I need it fixed before you go home.'

Rachel nodded along as her stepmother dragged her towards the stairs. 'Of course. Five minutes?' she said, twisting her neck to look over her shoulder at Damon.

'Take your time.' That easy smile was back. Of course he didn't mind, Rachel realised, as she made her way down the stairs to the ground floor. He got more flirting time with Gretchen and Maisie.

She wondered which one of them would win him over by the time she'd fixed the display.

Damon watched Rachel go, her knitted dress pulled tight across the curve of her backside, and wondered what on earth had possessed her to swap it for the hideous green velvet thing she'd been wearing when he arrived. Then he looked back at the predatory smiles on her stepsisters' faces and twigged.

'So you guys were helping Rachel choose a new dress?' he asked lightly as he headed over to a stack of discarded outfits on the chair by the door.

The one in the leather miniskirt—Maisie,

maybe?—nodded. 'For the company Christmas party,' she explained. 'Mum throws a huge one every year, and invites all the staff. It's so generous of her, really.'

'She told us that Rachel was planning on wearing the same old boring black dress she wears *every* year,' the other one—Gretchen, his mind filled in—went on. 'So *of course* we had to offer to help her find something better. It was our, well, *sisterly* duty.'

The girls exchanged a look that Damon pretended not to see. One that made his blood warm to a simmering boil on Rachel's behalf.

They weren't helping her, whatever they said. They were trying to humiliate her.

He knew how that felt—to be surrounded by people who thought they were smarter than him and thought he wouldn't notice when they used it against him. In his case, his family genuinely were cleverer; he didn't think the same of Rachel's stepsisters. All the same, he couldn't imagine Rachel liked it any more than he did.

Damon leafed through the pile of fabric. There were skimpy, showy outfits that he knew instinctively that Rachel would hate; oversized draping dresses in vile patterns and fabrics, that would cover every inch of Rachel's admirable curves; something that looked like a child's bridesmaid's dress in pink taffeta, complete with bow...all of them designed to make Rachel look ridiculous, he assumed.

She'd never been the show-off type, he remembered. Even next to his sister, who was always more likely to be found in the library than a nightclub, and prized the ability to quote Homer—the Ancient Greek writer, not the yellow cartoon figure, unfortunately, or else the siblings might have had more in common—high above the ability to put together a stylish outfit on a student budget. Rachel had been the one in the corner, tugging the sleeves of her cardigan over her hands, while Celeste got into an argument with someone about, well, pretty much anything. Rachel had been shy, quiet, mousy even, for all that he knew there was a dry sense of humour and a quick smile hiding behind those cardigans. And, as he'd discovered when crashing into her outside the bathroom one weekend when he was staying with them at university, when she was clad in nothing but a towel, some incredible curves.

He'd discovered more about her, one night— about her mind, her heart, her self. One night when it had been just the two of them, talking and dreaming aloud while they looked for Celeste together. One night, when he'd felt more of a connection to another person than he'd felt before or since.

But he tried not to think too often about that night. Not nine years ago, and definitely not now.

Because connection wasn't something Damon Hunter looked for in life.

The point was, the Rachel he'd known then, the Rachel he knew now, wouldn't wear any of these dresses willingly.

At the bottom of the pile, though, was something else. A quirky dress with woodland animals printed on it, in a great shade of dark red that would suit Rachel's colouring. 'Which one of you chose this one for her?' He pulled it out of the stack to get a better look. The neckline dipped into a low V-shape, it was tight through the bodice, then the skirt flared out to fall to, he imagined, around knee length. He smiled at the sight of the owls, stags and mice peeping out behind tree prints and fallen leaves.

It was, he had to admit, very Rachel. Maybe one of her stepsisters didn't have it in for her after all.

But when he looked up, Gretchen rolled her eyes. 'Oh, *that*. I picked that one up by accident— I was supposed to be putting it to one side for a client. I do personal shopping, you know. Helping people who have no idea of style to find things to make them look, well, less awful.'

'It's a nice dress,' Damon said, wondering how she could make shopping sound like a vocation *and* a way to humiliate people, all at the same time.

'Oh, but it would be *terrible* for Rachel—it would only draw attention to her, well, you know…' her voice dropped to a whisper '…*size.*'

Damon rather thought it would draw attention to her generous curves, which, in his opinion, could only be a good thing.

'I should put it away.' Gretchen reached out to take the dress from him, but Damon held it out of her reach as he checked the label. The size was the same as the other dresses in the stack, so it should fit her. And he'd bet money Celeste hadn't even thought about a Christmas present for her best friend yet. If he bought it, she could give it to Rachel as an early Christmas present, so she could wear it to the party. He'd have done a good deed, and he'd be in his sister's good books—hopefully good enough that she'd let him off Christmas shopping for their parents this year, since he never had any idea what to buy them anyway. Everybody won.

That was all. Nothing to do with that lingering connection he wasn't thinking about.

He flashed Gretchen and Maisie his most winning smile. They returned it, only for their faces to fall as he said, 'I think I'll buy it for her. Are there any tills still open?'

There weren't, but it only took a little fast talk

and a few smiles to find an employee willing to put the sale through for him anyway—with their staff discount, to boot, not that he needed it. Then, leaving the stepsisters behind with their hideous dress choices, Damon took his Hartbury & Sons designer paper bag and ambled towards the ground floor window displays to find Rachel.

It took him longer than he'd expected. The storefront stretched around the corner to front onto two streets, giving it six huge windows to look out over the pavement. With the main lighting switched off for the night, and only a few spotlights left on to illuminate things for the cleaning staff, he had to check each window individually to locate Rachel, and even then he missed her. Only when he'd peered into all six windows without spotting her did he head back to the centre and call out.

'Rach?'

A torchlight beam swung around from the far window and caught him in the eyes. Blinking, he covered them with his hand, just as he saw Rachel clambering out from behind the window display in the first window he'd checked. God only knew where she'd managed to hide, but between the decorations and some sort of backboard, it was hard to get a good look in there.

'Sorry, sorry. Are we late?' she asked, switching off the torch.

'Not if you're ready to go now.' And if he drove just a tiny bit faster than was strictly advisable on winter city streets.

'I am, I am.' Grabbing her bag from the floor by the window, she rushed towards the door, half colliding with him on her way, which only served to make her more flustered. 'Sorry!'

With a smile, Damon calmly took Rachel's elbow and led her in the direction of the exit.

She'd always been like this, he reflected. The day he'd met her she'd managed to dump half the cup of tea she'd just made over herself, the floor, and the biscuit tin as he'd walked into the kitchen and Celeste had introduced them. Rachel was Rachel—a little shy, a lot clumsy. She still wore the same, oversized knits she'd worn at university too, and her hair still curled around her face the same way. She was a constant; he'd almost call her part of the family if that wasn't actually an insult, given his family. He *had* to put up with them. What made Rachel put up with Celeste he'd never been entirely sure.

He had a pretty good idea what Celeste got from being friends with Rachel, though. On his bad days, it made him a little jealous.

'So, what happened to the window display that couldn't wait until morning?' he asked.

Rachel pulled a face, still looking frazzled. He supposed her evening so far couldn't have been the most fun: playing dress up with her stepsisters, then having to fix the window. He hadn't stopped to look at the Christmas displays on the way in, but these things were all much of a muchness, right? Bit of tinsel, a fake tree, a mannequin wearing a Christmas jumper and some boxes covered in wrapping paper. Much like the vignettes littering the inside of the shop—and Damon was pretty sure he wouldn't have noticed them at all if it weren't for the latest project he'd taken on, occupying his brain.

'Hannah was right, it was all my fault. It was the mice, you see. Too tempting, I suppose.'

'Mice?' Where did they fit into the Christmas theme? Or were these the same mice he saw scuttling about on the London Underground, on the rare occasions he travelled on it?

'Come on. I'll show you.' As they left via the side door, she dragged him around to the furthest window. 'Can you see the mouse?'

Damon blinked as he took in the display. Not a string of tinsel to be seen, although there were plenty of fairy lights, illuminating the scene for passers-by.

There were no mannequins in Christmas jumpers either, or fake presents. Instead, the window opened up onto another world filled with what looked like a whole village made of gingerbread—iced houses and shops with tiny

Christmas cakes and cookies for sale behind their windows. There was a Christmas tree, of course—two, in fact. One was made from a giant stack of gingerbread stars, with iced decorations and pinprick fairy lights. The other was actually a tower of perfect white iced Christmas cakes, stacked from biggest to smallest, with a golden iced, star-shaped cake on top.

In between the trees, in front of the buildings and surrounded by icing-sugar snow, was a mirror lake with an ice-skating hedgehog, rabbit and even a deer with tiny skates on all four hooves. But no mouse.

'I don't see it,' he admitted, peering harder.

Rachel grinned. 'Then I've done it right. Try getting down to child level.'

Giving her a sceptical look, Damon squatted down closer to the pavement—and suddenly the scene took on a whole new dimension.

He'd assumed that the shop windows, with their tiny fake treats, were all there was to the buildings. He'd been wrong. From this level—the level at which the shop's younger visitors would be viewing it—he could see far more. Behind the windows there were whole new worlds: decorated living rooms, shops with tiny animal customers, and there, curled up on an armchair by a Christmas tree, a small mouse. 'I see him!'

Even Damon could hear the delight in his

voice, and it made Rachel's smile widen further. 'There's a mouse in every window,' she explained. 'Hidden, as a sort of treasure hunt for the kids.'

'Are they all like this?' He looked back at the astonishing display. 'Because this is amazing. Did you do this?' Of course she had. It was total Rachel—nice to look at on the surface, but with so much more to offer underneath.

*Stop thinking about it.* He mentally pulled away from thinking about Rachel, even as she was standing beside him. It was easy enough. He'd had years of practice.

Unaware of his roving thoughts, Rachel ducked her chin modestly. 'Yeah. I do them every year. It's kind of my thing. But they're not all exactly like this; this one is for our food and drink gifting range. There's one for womenswear, one for homewares, one for kids' gifts…' She shrugged. 'Basically, I split the six windows to cover all the big areas of the store.'

'Can I see them?' In the back of his mind an idea was forming. One that had nothing to do with spending more time with Rachel, and everything to do with business. Just as it should be.

If all her window displays were as cool as this one, Rachel could be just what he needed to get his latest project working at last.

'Have we got time? Won't Celeste be waiting?'

Rachel's teeth pressed against her plump lower lip, a line of concern forming between her brows.

Damon flashed her his best 'Trust Me' smile. 'Celeste can wait. I want to see your work.'

Spots of pink appeared in her cheeks, and he knew the smile had worked its usual magic. 'Okay. Come this way.'

# CHAPTER TWO

IT WAS ANOTHER twenty minutes before Rachel eased herself into the passenger seat of Damon's flashy sports car. She had no idea of the make—cars weren't exactly her thing—but, knowing Damon as she did, it would be the most expensive, and the fastest.

He'd seemed oddly charmed by her window displays, she mused as he started the engine. She hadn't exactly imagined that Damon Hunter, entrepreneur and all-round playboy, would find much to admire in her tiny scenes of festive fun. But he had.

It had been a long time since she'd seen beneath the charming, suave exterior of the perfect businessman that Damon projected to the world—not since they were both teenagers. And even then, there'd only been one night where she thought she'd glimpsed the real boy behind the facade.

The fact that just that one night had been enough to fuel an almost decade-long crush was beside the point. Rachel had been fairly sure that, as he'd grown up, that boy had faded away. But his delight at her whimsical window displays made her wonder if he'd really disappeared after all.

'So you do those windows every year?' he asked now, as he eased the car out of its dubiously legal parking spot and into the central London traffic.

'Yep. It's kind of my thing.' Something to look forward to in between the monotony of shifts on the tills or on the floor of the department store.

Working at Hartbury & Sons hadn't exactly been her dream career when she'd been studying English at university in Oxford with Celeste. But then, if she'd actually had any idea what her dream career was, maybe she'd have made more effort to go after it.

And as her dad pointed out, there weren't many family businesses on the scale of Hartbury's still going these days. It was good that they were part of the tradition—even if it wasn't technically her family tradition at all.

'And do you do them for other stores too, or just your stepmother's?'

Rachel blinked in surprise. 'Uh…just for Hartbury's. I mean, it's part of my job. Working there.'

'I thought Celeste said you were doing marketing and social media these days? You know, freelancing, like me.'

She couldn't help the snort of laughter that

burst out of her; for all she knew it was probably one of the least attractive sounds in the universe. 'Celeste exaggerated.'

'So what do you do, exactly?'

Why did he even care? Rachel couldn't imagine, but she shrugged and answered all the same. 'I work on the shop floor, on the tills, putting out stock, that sort of thing. Everyone has to put in time there when we're busy, especially at Christmas. But I'm also in charge of the window displays and I run the social media and keep the website updated—not the online shop, but the blog and stuff.'

It sounded almost impressive when she listed it out. The Hartbury & Sons social media accounts had exploded since she took them over, especially since she started posting photos of the window displays, and the blog got a decent number of hits too. She'd managed to talk her stepmother into coughing up for some online training for her, and the shop was seeing the benefits of her newfound expertise.

But it didn't *feel* impressive. Not when she was still living at home, suffering the petty meanness of her stepsisters, and the way her father never seemed able to see it. Not compared to Celeste's high-flying academic career and TV appearances. Not compared to Damon's business success. She didn't even pretend to understand exactly what it was his company did, beyond what Celeste had told her.

*'Companies that are doing badly get him in, and suddenly they're in profit again. He's like a business wizard, I think.'*

But whatever it was, he was clearly very successful at it. Even Celeste sounded proud of him—not that Rachel imagined her best friend would ever tell him so.

It didn't even feel particularly impressive compared to her own vague hopes and dreams for her career. She'd never found a way to articulate what it was she really wanted from her employment, but in the back of her mind she'd always known how it would feel.

She'd be in charge of her own work; she'd have control over her schedule. Probably working from home, doing something creative that fulfilled her. Maybe even being her own boss. The one who decided what she did and when.

Working at Hartbury's definitely didn't give her that.

*One step at a time*, she reminded herself. *Dad gets the all-clear from the docs, then I move out. Then I can think about my potential career.*

It was how she'd got through everything else in life—her mother's death, her father's unexpected remarriage, being a member of a new blended family she never really felt part of, being an outsider again at Oxford, and everything since. One step at a time.

Damon, she suspected, would hop, skip and jump all over the place as the whim took him. He'd never had the patience to plod along like her.

'What's your favourite part of the job?' Damon asked, and there was genuine curiosity in his voice. It warmed her a little to think he cared enough to ask.

Nobody else did, it seemed. Even her father just told her he was glad she was doing so well working for the family business without ever asking her if it was what she wanted, or giving her a chance to tell him it wasn't, before he went on about his day.

*He's got a lot on his mind*, she told herself sternly. Ever since his suspected heart attack he'd been preoccupied, obviously worrying. Just like her.

*But even before then he just assumed you liked working at Hartbury's*, a nagging, alternative voice reminded her.

She shook it away. Her father had his faults, but she loved him anyway. He was her only real family since her mother died when she was twelve. And if he'd rushed into another marriage, another family, just a couple of years later, she knew well enough why he'd done it.

*For me. He wanted to give me a family again.*

She'd never had the heart to tell him that, as the years had passed, she'd felt less a part of a family with Hannah and the girls than she'd felt when it was just the two of them. How could she when he was trying so hard? And then, by the time she'd accepted that she would never be a real part of Hannah's family, she'd recognised that her dad already was. She'd lost her mother, and she couldn't risk losing him too by walking away from that new family.

Damon was still waiting for a response, she realised. What did he want to know? Her favourite part of the job...

'I like doing the windows,' she said slowly, thinking. Never having been asked before, she'd not really thought about the answer. 'They're fun and creative and I like seeing the kids' faces when they spot them.'

'But they're not your favourites?' A traffic light turned green and Damon instantly pressed the accelerator and sped forward over a brief patch of empty road, changing lanes at speed.

'I... I think I like the social media side of it more, actually. I didn't think I would—I mean, communicating with people has never exactly been my strong point.' She shot him a wry smile, and his gaze darted from the road to meet hers for a moment. He didn't contradict her, which she appreciated. Too often her family spoke over her, telling the story of her life as they saw it—or as they wanted to see it—rather than the one she was actually living. Being allowed to narrate her own life story was strangely liberating.

Or maybe he was remembering that one night where they'd talked almost until morning. *Stop thinking about it, Rachel.* That was a long time ago, and it wasn't as if it had led anywhere anyway.

'What do you love about it?' Damon swung the car around a corner into a darkened street between two much taller buildings. Rachel couldn't help but wonder how he knew his way around the city so well by car. She was reasonable enough at finding her way via the Tube, or on foot, at least in areas she knew. But she'd never even *tried* to drive in the city. It didn't seem to faze Damon, though.

But then, nothing really did. Even when he was a newly turned eighteen-year-old hanging out in their university flat, mostly to avoid being at home with his parents as far as Rachel could tell. Even then he'd had more confidence, more charm, than Rachel had ever dreamt of.

It was the kind of confidence she saw in some of her fellow students—usually the ones who had money, or whose family name and title went back generations. The sort of confidence you had to inherit.

Heaven only knew where Damon had got it, coming from the same family as Celeste. The Doctors Hunter, she knew from one awkward holiday visit, were academics, not aristocracy. They were well off enough, for sure, with a London town house many would envy. But while they, and Celeste, were always confident in their academic knowledge and their ability to be right, none of them had any talent for small talk or winning people over by force of personality rather than facts.

Apparently Damon had got all the charm in the family. And boy did he know how to use it. He'd brought enough university students back to their flat for her to be sure of that.

'So?' He swung the car into a tiny parking space between two SUVs without even setting off the parking sensors. 'What is it you love about social media?'

'Um…' Rachel tried to find the words to explain it, but before she could talk her phone started ringing loudly in her bag. Fumbling, she pulled it out. 'Celeste,' she explained, showing him his sister's name on the screen.

'Where are you?' Celeste asked, as soon as she answered. 'We're starting filming any minute!'

'We're here, we're here.' Rachel opened the car door, trying not to crash into the neighbouring car as she tumbled out. 'We'll be there any second now, I promise.'

'Okay. Hurry!'

'You can tell me later.' Damon nonchalantly clicked the button to lock the car, and strolled towards the entrance as if there were no rush at all. Rachel couldn't help but watch him go.

Wow, but he'd grown up well. He'd been gorgeous at eighteen, but these days he was something else. Broad at the shoulder, narrow at the waist and strong, muscular legs, she could tell, even through his suit trousers. The lamplight flickered on his dark hair. He looked like the final scene of a movie, walking away like that.

'Come on,' he called back over his shoulder, and Rachel hurried to catch up.

She wasn't wasting time on that daydream any longer. She had her own plodding plans to follow.

*One step at a time.*

Well, this was hideous.

Damon loved his sister, really he did, but that didn't make him blind to her many, many flaws. Most obviously right now, an inability to back down from an argument when she was convinced she was right.

The fact that she was always, always right hadn't made this trait any easier to bear during his childhood years and, right now, it didn't look as if it was making the situation easier for media darling Theo Montgomery, who had the bad luck to be hosting the Christmas Cracker Cranium Quiz.

'All I'm saying is that the answer you have on that card is incomplete and gives the audience an incorrect view about Christmas traditions,' Celeste said, her arms folded across the sparkly Christmas jumper Damon was certain had been foisted on her by the wardrobe department. He'd definitely never seen his big sister wear anything so…seasonal before. Or anything that wasn't black or white, for that matter. Celeste lived in monochrome. Colour, it seemed, was too distracting from her aims of being right, being clever, and climbing the academic ladder at the London university where she, and both their parents, worked.

Beside him in the audience, Rachel was visibly cringing, as if she were trying to disappear into her knitted dress. He couldn't blame her. This was excruciating.

He'd known it was going to go badly from the moment they'd arrived. Celeste had been waiting for them, just inside the building, wearing that incongruous sweater over her black jeans and tapping her foot impatiently.

'What took you so long?' she'd asked, grabbing Rachel's arm and pulling her into step with her. 'Let me guess, Damon was flirting with your stepsisters?'

He couldn't see Rachel's face to gauge her re-action to that, but he imagined she was smiling. After all, that was what he did, wasn't it? Flirt with pretty women in an irresponsible manner that resulted in him being late. If she were asked, he reckoned Celeste would say that was a reason-able assassination of his character.

But to his surprise, Rachel had defended him. 'Actually, it was my fault. I had to fix a window display before we left.'

She didn't mention that he'd then insisted on looking at all of them, and that that was what had actually made them late. He'd wondered why, but had put it down to Rachel just being nice like that.

Now, watching Celeste and Theo go at it again over the correct pronunciation of the answer to what was only question five of a half-hour show, he figured she just hadn't wanted to rile Celeste up any more than necessary. Not that it seemed to have helped.

'Isn't this supposed to be a "light-hearted, in-tellectual festive quiz"?' Rachel asked, leaning close to whisper in his ear. Her hair smelled like something Christmassy although he couldn't quite put his finger on exactly what. Something spicy, though. He liked it.

'That's what she told Mum and Dad at Sunday lunch the other week,' he murmured back. 'Of course, that didn't make them any more enamoured with the idea of her doing it.' They'd never really approved of any of Celeste's TV, radio or podcast appearances, not even the classics-for-the-masses documentary ones. Not academic enough for them, apparently. Much like Damon himself.

Maybe he and Celeste could have bonded over it, if she hadn't still been a thousand times closer to being their perfect child than he could ever hope to be.

Not that he wanted to be any more.

'This does not feel light-hearted.' Even in her whispered tone, he could hear how heartfelt that was. Rachel, he remembered, didn't like conflict. Presumably that was why she let her stepsisters walk all over her the way they seemed to. He couldn't imagine why else she wouldn't take a stand against their petty meanness.

Up on set, Theo made a joke that made the other contestants laugh nervously. Celeste just glowered at him some more.

He'd known that Theo and his sister were going to clash from the moment they'd entered the studio. Celeste might have fancy make-up on and her hair done in artful curls in a way she'd never bother to do herself, but underneath she was still the girl he'd grown up with. The big sister who could never let anything lie, could never move on from a fight without him admitting that she'd been right all along. The one who wrote long, persuasive essays then read them out to their parents to convince them to do things her way.

So when Theo had swept over to introduce himself, TV-star smile in place, all easy friendliness and 'let's all just get along and have some fun' vibes, Damon had *known* that he and Celeste were going to hate each other. True to form, from the moment he'd shaken Theo's hand, Celeste had been glaring at the presenter.

He could almost hear her thoughts: *Too suave, too smooth, only here because of his face and his name*—because who didn't know that Theo Montgomery was one of *those* Montgomerys?—*and doesn't know anything about the subjects we'll be answering questions on.*

If there was anything Celeste hated more than people thinking she was wrong, it was people who thought they were right when actually they just didn't understand the argument. Sometimes, they didn't even know they were arguing in the first place, but, in the Hunter family, everything was either a competition or an argument. Often both.

He suspected Theo had foreseen the potential clash too because he'd turned the charm up another couple of notches. A bad move because, as Damon could have predicted, it only made his sister bristle more. Celeste hated people who were all style and no substance.

Damon assumed his sister tolerated him because he was family. Or maybe because Rachel had told her she had to. Sometimes he thought Celeste's friendship with Rachel was the only thing that had stopped his sister turning into their parents years ago.

The bristling between Theo and Celeste had now apparently turned into televised warfare. Damon had no idea how anybody was going to edit this to make it a 'light-hearted festive quiz' to air in the weeks before Christmas. He was just very glad it wasn't his job.

The director called for a break after the latest set of questions, and the whole studio audience gave a sigh of relief. Damon suspected that someone would be talking to his sister right now about appropriate quiz-show behaviour.

He'd have done it himself, but at that moment he spotted a young woman with a clipboard making her way along the rows of the audience, talking to people as she went—and those audience members getting up and walking out of the studio.

Hmm. Was that because of Celeste or something else?

'Hang on,' he said to Rachel, and vaulted over the empty front-row seats to accost the girl with the clipboard. If there was something else more interesting going on somewhere, he wanted in.

Or, more specifically, out of this passive-aggressive rerun of all his worst childhood dinners.

And if he was getting out, he was taking Rachel with him.

Damon returned, smiling broadly, accompanied by a besotted-looking production assistant with a clipboard. The poor girl had spent barely three minutes in his company and she already looked half in love.

It was somewhat reassuring to know he had that effect on everybody, not just Rachel.

Right now, however, she was starting to worry he'd lost his mind.

'They want us to…what?' Rachel frowned, running his words through her mind again. They still didn't make any sense.

'Bring in the new year with a bang!' Damon said, beaming.

'Now?'

'Yep.'

'On the…' she checked the date dial on her watch to make sure she wasn't imagining things '…first of December?'

'Apparently so!' Damon was still grinning at the idea, so Rachel turned to the girl with the clipboard for some sort of explanation.

'We're filming our New Year's Eve countdown and party show a few doors down,' the assistant said. 'But there's some sort of problem on the Tube, and half our booked partygoers haven't shown up, so we're recruiting volunteers from other studio audiences right now.'

Rachel blinked. 'Wait. Is this the countdown show that goes out live on New Year's Eve? You know, the one that, well, counts down to midnight?'

The girl's pupils slid sideways as she broke eye contact. 'We never actually *say* it's live.'

'Come on, Rach, you didn't really think all those celebrities they have on had nothing better to do on New Year's Eve than hang out in a TV studio with the ordinary people, did you?' Damon asked.

It could have sounded cruel, mocking, and maybe from someone else it would. But Damon, standing just about far enough behind the production assistant that she couldn't see his face, followed up his words by widening his eyes, shrugging, and mouthing, *'Me neither.'*

Rachel stifled a laugh. 'Well, obviously not. So what would we have to do, exactly?'

The production assistant—the access card on the lanyard around her neck said her name was Amy—shrugged. 'Just, well, you know. Party. Dance. Have fun.' She looked Rachel up and down, and she could feel her taking in her oversized knit dress, her mostly make-up-free face, and her curls with a clear headband shoved in them to keep them out of her face. 'Do you think you can manage that?'

*No.*

Partying wasn't exactly her sort of thing. Even at university she and Celeste had been more the 'cups of tea and watching a movie on a Friday night' sort of students. In fact, the only parties she remembered them going to were ones Damon had somehow got them invited to during his regular visits.

*Like the one where we lost Celeste and spent all night together looking for her... Not thinking about it.*

The point was, she wanted to party. Even at university she'd *wanted* to get out there and meet new people. She just hadn't had—still didn't have—the confidence to try, and staying in with Celeste had been more comfortable and less stressful all round.

She should stay and support Celeste now in this show, however excruciating it was to watch her battling with the host. Somewhere in the back of her mind, though, a long-silenced voice was screaming at her to go. To have fun. To dance and party with Damon, just as she'd wanted to at eighteen.

Rachel ignored the voice, as usual. It wasn't in the plan.

Damon, however, had other ideas.

'Of course she can!' he said, gleefully. Grabbing her hand, he tugged her around the row of seats he'd vaulted over, then wrapped an arm around her shoulder to hold her close against him. 'You should have seen this one party at university! Trust me, she's an animal!'

Amy the production assistant looked understandably dubious. Damon gave Rachel's shoulder a little shake, and she forced a smile. 'I'd love to help with the New Year countdown show,' she said.

It felt as if the words were coming from another person's mouth. Or as if she were a puppet, controlled by Damon, saying something she'd never imagined saying in real life. If she'd ever let Damon drag her along to such a thing she'd have always made it clear it wasn't her idea so if it went horribly wrong she could duck out of any responsibility, or anyone thinking she'd believed for a moment she could do it in the first place.

But no, something had made her actually say what she wanted to do, and take responsibility for it.

She had a suspicion it was the way Damon was pressed up against her side, the fresh scent of his aftershave filling her every breath, and her whole body tingling with awareness of his closeness. Clearly his proximity had messed with her neural network, the part that made thoughts into words. It was the only explanation.

'Well, great,' Amy said, marking down another tally on her clipboard to add to the others from the audience. Then she paused, and looked up at Rachel again. 'Um… I don't suppose you have something more…partyish you could wear, do you? I mean, I can see if anyone's free in hair and make-up to help with that, but I'm not sure whether wardrobe will have anything… *appropriate*.'

She meant in the right size, Rachel realised. Most of the shows filmed here seemed to feature those perfect size-six women, and Rachel was happy to admit she wasn't that.

She was short, curvy and healthy. Normally, that was enough for her. But here and now…she looked around the rest of the audience, queuing to take part in the New Year party—probably as an escape from the festive quiz show from hell. They all seemed to have dressed up rather more for the occasion than she'd thought to. Her usual policy was to wear clothes that enabled her to fade into the background. After all, if no one was going to notice her, it didn't much matter what she wore.

But if she was going to be on TV—actually on TV, not just sitting in the audience next to

Damon, who would draw everyone's attention anyway—then suddenly her comfy old jumper dress and leggings didn't feel entirely appropriate. Especially not for what was supposed to be the party of the year.

She was about to back out again, to claim that she really had to stay and support Celeste after all, when Damon said, 'Don't worry, I've got that covered. Just need to grab it from the car. Hang on.'

Rachel watched as he eased his way through the queue with grace and charm, smiling and chatting as he went, and out through the door back to the car park. When he was gone, she turned back to Amy, who was still looking puzzled by this whole turn of events.

'I don't have any idea what he has planned, but I suspect I'm going to need to take you up on that offer of hair and make-up.'

Amy beamed. 'Follow me.'

# CHAPTER THREE

WHEN DAMON RETURNED from his trip to the car, he found Amy waiting for him—and Rachel nowhere to be seen.

'Is that her outfit?' Amy grabbed the bag from him without waiting for much of an answer. 'Great. I'll give it to her. You head through there and help yourself to a drink; they're almost ready to start.'

Ambling into the studio, Damon took a glass of something sparkling from a waiter circulating with a tray, and surveyed the crowd. It was easy enough to see who had planned to be here and who had been drafted in at the last minute. The original female partygoers all wore the kind of sparkly sequinned dresses and heels he'd expect at a swanky New Year's Eve party, while the men were in dinner jackets or smart suits. The last-minute additions were more casually dressed, although most had at least dressed up for their visit to the studios anyway, so there weren't many jeans or trainers to be seen.

His work suit stood up well enough, he decided, and the dress he'd bought for Rachel would be fine too—even if it meant Celeste would now have to find her own Christmas present for her best friend.

The studio itself was party ready too. On the main stage area was a giant digital clock, ticking inexorably down towards fictional midnight. Right now, it seemed to think it was around ten-thirty at night, rather than, as his watch told him, not quite eight o'clock. There was a Christmas tree in the corner, decked out with tasteful decorations and lights—although no kind of display at all compared to Rachel's windows. Cocktail-bar-style high tables had been set up around the perimeter, allowing people to gather in small groups and chat. He spotted a couple of assistants with the same clipboard-and-microphone-headset ensemble as Amy darting around encouraging people to mingle. It seemed they wanted this place to look like an actual party—right down to the dance floor in front of the stage.

A band was setting up on the stage itself—a big band, the kind that played classic swing music—and every now and then a few bars of one of the Rat Pack's greatest hits would boom out across the party. The host—a well-known TV personality—was chatting with the director off to one side of the stage. Damon was surprised that Theo Montgomery, the host of the quiz show Celeste was appearing on, hadn't been tagged for the role, until he remembered that of course Theo would be doing the *actual* live broadcast on New Year's Eve. It would ruin the illusion to have him in two places at once.

Still, if Damon knew his sister—and he did—he'd bet that Theo would rather be here with a glass of warm sparkling wine than asking Celeste questions and having to deal with her dissatisfaction with the answers.

One of the assistants clapped his hands, obviously trying to get everyone's attention before filming. But Damon wasn't really listening. Because, at that moment, the door to the studio opened again and Rachel walked in.

*I was right about the dress*, was his first thought. It clung perfectly to those glorious curves she usually hid away, dipping to a slight vee at the front to give shape without being revealing enough to make her self-conscious, he hoped. The skirt swirled around her legs to her knees, above the same ankle boots she'd been wearing earlier. The woodland animals in the pattern almost seemed to dance around under the studio lights, peeping around the tree print on the fabric. It reminded him of the magical window displays she'd created, he realised.

Maybe that was why he couldn't stop looking at her. Sure, the hair and make-up team had done stuff to her hair and face but, to be honest, he'd always thought Rachel looked lovely without all that. And even her fabulous figure wasn't a surprise; he'd always known it was there. He just hadn't spent much time thinking about it lately.

Now, watching her cross the room towards him, he couldn't think about anything else.

'You look fantastic,' he said, the words a little hoarse as they made their way out of his suddenly dry throat.

'I can't believe you bought this dress—how lucky was that? Who was it for?' Rachel glanced down at the dress, her fingers holding out the skirt a little as she studied the pattern. 'It's so cute.'

'It was for you,' he said, honestly. Rachel looked up sharply, that frown line back between her eyebrows. 'I saw it in the pile of dresses you'd been trying on and, well, it was the only one that actually looked like *you*. So I bought it. I figured Celeste might like to give it to you for Christmas, or something.'

It had seemed like a perfectly normal impulse when he'd done it, but now he had to explain his reasoning he wasn't so sure. Neither was Rachel, by the look of things.

'That was…kind of you.' Kind was better than weird, right? He'd take it.

'It looks a bit like your windows,' he said.

Rachel beamed. 'That's what I thought when I saw it! But Gretchen said it would draw too much attention to my, well…size.'

'Trust me,' Damon said, with feeling, 'it's drawing exactly the right amount of attention to your figure. You look incredible.' And he really had to stop looking at his big sister's best friend that way. Not least because she'd never given him even the slightest hint that she wanted him to.

*There was that one night*, his brain reminded him. *That one night when you could have kissed her, if you'd wanted to.*

But he hadn't. Because she was Celeste's best friend. Because she wasn't the sort of girl you messed around with, and he hadn't known how to do anything else.

Because she'd seen deeper than he liked, and it had scared him.

Her smile turned shy and she went back to studying the creatures on her dress, thankfully oblivious to his thoughts. 'It *is* like my windows, isn't it?'

Somewhere someone clapped their hands again, and bellowed for them to take their places.

'Come on. We're starting.' Damon took her arm and led her towards the bar. He needed another drink, and she hadn't even had one yet. 'Let's grab a glass of something bubbly, and you can tell me more about your windows and your work until it's time to shout out the countdown, or whatever we need to do.'

'You really want to know more about the windows?' She sounded astonished at the prospect.

'As it happens, I really, really do.' And not just because of the way she lit up when she spoke about the things that mattered to her. Or because it would give him a chance to listen to her melodious voice. Those things weren't important to him. Or shouldn't be anyway.

No, he wanted to know more because he had the inklings of an idea that could help *both* of them get what they needed in life. If he could persuade her to take a chance on him.

It was just business. That was all.

He needed to keep reminding himself of that.

'And it's ten minutes to midnight!' the host bellowed as the band finished its latest song and the crowd whooped loudly. The free sparkling wine had been flowing merrily, and the last-minute partygoers had definitely been taking advantage of it.

'Funny,' Damon murmured. 'It only feels like quarter past nine.'

Rachel hid a grin behind her hand as one of the cameramen swooped past. 'Yeah, this is weird.'

Except somehow it really wasn't. Oh, the whole

'pretend it's actually December the thirty-first' thing was wacky as anything, but being with Damon for the night? That wasn't nearly as weird as she'd expected it to be when Celeste had told her he'd be there tonight too, and that was when she'd thought they'd just be sitting next to each other in the audience for the quiz show.

She felt a pang of guilt about abandoning her best friend, but pushed it aside. There was no way she'd have been able to sit through an hour or more of Celeste and Theo Montgomery verbally sparring anyway. If Amy the production assistant hadn't asked them to join the party filming when she did, Rachel had already been planning an emergency escape to the loos, and maybe getting lost on the way back. Conflict really wasn't her thing.

Hanging out with Damon at the fake party was a lot more fun than pretending to lose her way in the TV studio's corridors.

He'd meant it when he said he wanted to talk more about her windows. And not just the window displays; he'd asked more questions about her job, her career ambitions, her hopes and dreams, than anybody else had, ever. Not her family, not even Celeste—although, in fairness, that was mostly because Rachel had been shutting down conversations about what she wanted from life for so long now that Celeste had stopped even asking.

She knew her best friend meant well, but it was hard to talk about maybe possibly taking on some freelance clients who she could run social media accounts for as an actual career path, when Celeste's academic ladder was so well scaled already.

But with Damon…somehow, the fact that he was rich and successful didn't intimidate her the way his sister's success did. Perhaps because he was so casual about it compared to Celeste's laser focus. As if he was just doing what was fun, and what he was good at, and it all worked out rather well—although she suspected there had to be more to it than that, no matter how relaxed he was talking about his own business.

It had been fascinating spending this evening with him, seeing the man he'd grown into rather than the boy she remembered. They hadn't spent much time together in the years since she'd left university, and definitely not alone. In fact, in almost ten years of acquaintance, there was only one night where it had been just the two of them.

One night that was seared into her memory, even though nothing had happened.

Suddenly she needed to know if Damon remembered it too.

'Do you remember that night at university where we went to that party in our college and lost Celeste?'

It was just a casual question, a reminiscence of sorts. There was no reason for Damon to freeze up as suddenly as he did at her words.

Or maybe she imagined it, because a moment later he was smiling, his shoulders loose and relaxed again.

'She showed up in the library, didn't she?' he said.

Rachel nodded. 'She'd had an idea about her essay and the library was still just about open, so she'd snuck over to check her sources or something.'

'And got locked in,' Damon added. 'While we scoured the college—and the city—looking for her.'

'Yeah.' She met his gaze, and just for a second she could believe that he remembered that night the same way she did. As an unforgettable interlude in an otherwise boring life.

Except, of course, Damon's life was anything but boring. He probably stayed up all night and talked about his innermost dreams and feelings with people all the time. Back then, she'd hoped him opening up to her that way, listening to her talk about her own life, meant she was special. Now she realised, with the hindsight of age, he was probably that way with everyone. He had friends all over the world, and a whole list of women desperate to spend the night with him—and do a lot more than talk.

While she had Celeste, and her family. And tonight.

Which wasn't nothing.

'Do you think we're supposed to be going somewhere?' Rachel asked, suddenly uncomfortably aware that all the other partygoers seemed to be congregating on the dance floor.

'Apparently so.' Damon got to his feet and held a hand out to her just as the band struck up another tune—a fast, fun, reeling jig of a tune that had even Rachel's reluctant toes tapping.

She didn't dance. She *couldn't* dance. She'd been thrown out of junior ballet for her total inability, and hadn't ever danced since. She'd avoided it at every nightclub, every party, every wedding she'd ever attended.

Now she was expected to dance on not-even-a-little-bit-live TV. With Damon Hunter.

And the absolute weirdest part of all was that she *wanted* to. Because it was Damon. She'd never have sought out this opportunity, never even hoped for it, but now it was here...even though every bit of her emotional muscle memory was screaming at her to turn it down, to fall back on her usual *'Actually, I'm happier just watching'* line, she didn't.

Her stomach clenching with nerves, Rachel

took his hand and followed him onto the dance floor, ignoring all the bits of her brain that were telling her what a terrible idea this was.

'It's ages since I've had a night out dancing,' Damon said, pulling her into his arms. Rachel tried desperately to remember where her hands were supposed to go—no, definitely not *there*, she reminded herself as she recalled how good his backside looked in his suit trousers—and was relieved when he took one of hers in his larger hand, entwining his fingers with hers, and rested the other at her waist.

The music had changed. When had the music changed? Probably while she was agonising over whether she could even remember how to dance, and the fact that most of her dance experience was actually just watching *Dirty Dancing* too many times as an impressionable teen. Either way, the lively, jive-like music had faded into something more sultry. Not slow, exactly, but definitely sexy. Definitely intended to get the audience up close and personal before the fake midnight gongs.

As the music instructed, Damon tugged her a little closer, one big hand at the small of her back, the other still holding hers. They must look ridiculous; she was more than a head and a half shorter than him, even in her low-heeled boots. If she wanted to see his face she'd have to crane her neck right back. As it was, she was mostly staring at his nicely muscled chest in his white shirt, trying not to imagine undoing the buttons.

'Okay?' Damon murmured, somewhere around the top of her head, and she felt the word vibrating through that very fine chest.

'Mmm-hmm.' She didn't trust herself to speak actual words at the moment. When would this song be over? She'd *known* dancing was a bad idea. She had no idea what her feet were doing, her hips were probably swaying far too much but she couldn't seem to stop them, and her face ached from smiling stiffly in case the cameras caught them.

'Only, you're gripping a little tight there, you know,' Damon said, casually.

Rachel's eyes widened as she looked down and saw his suit jacket fisted in her fingers. That suit was probably worth more than her entire wardrobe, and here she was scrunching it up. The only reason her other hand wasn't doing the same was probably because it was in his, and she was scrupulously trying to avoid touching him any more than necessary.

An endeavour that was promptly ruined by Damon himself. Taking his hand from the small of her back, he peeled her fingers away from his suit jacket, all while still moving in time to the music. Then, he placed her hand under his suit jacket, resting just above his hip, so she could feel the warmth of his skin through his thin shirt.

Oh, this was such a bad idea...

She glanced up. He was smirking. 'Better?'

'For your suit, I suppose,' she said, amazed she could find any words at all.

He chuckled, replacing his palm against her spine and sending a shiver all the way up it.

She'd never been this close to him before. And now, all she could think was that she might never be this close again.

Last time they'd been alone together for a night, they'd just talked. This time... Rachel couldn't help but imagine so much more.

All those repressed impulses she'd spent so many years ignoring bubbled up inside her, as if loosening up enough to dance had given them all the same hope of a way out. The possibility that she'd suddenly start taking chances she'd always swerved away from before.

She wouldn't, of course. But that knowledge wasn't enough to stop her thinking about them. Wondering what would happen if she just...gave in, and asked for what she wanted for a change.

One dance and she was thinking about breaking a lifetime of caution, reticence and wallflowerness. Heaven help her if Damon ever actually showed any interest in her.

*Don't think about it. Especially not now, when you're in the man's arms, for heaven's sake.*

But she *was* thinking about it. In fact, as the song finished, and the host grabbed the microphone again to start the ten-second countdown to fake midnight, it was all she *could* think about.

They'd stopped moving with the music, naturally, but they hadn't moved apart at all. Rachel tilted her chin up to look into his bright blue eyes.

'Five,' he whispered, and a buzzy feeling started somewhere in her chest.

'Four,' she said, her hoarse voice almost lost amongst the shouting. All around them, people were preparing for midnight, acting up for the cameras, and Rachel knew they should be too. But she couldn't look away from Damon's blue, blue eyes…

'Three. Two. One!' The crowd cheered, the confetti came down, Big Ben chimed midnight— presumably recorded—and it was officially a new year, a fresh start, a chance to do things differently…even if it was all pretend.

If it was all pretend, none of this would count tomorrow, right? It could all be forgotten. A dream, a fairy tale. Something that happened to another girl in another world.

That was what Rachel was telling herself anyway, as the band broke into the introduction to 'Auld Lang Syne', and she stretched up on her tiptoes, her mouth tantalisingly close to Damon's as he dipped his head towards her.

'Happy New Year,' she murmured. Every muscle in her body was tensed, waiting for what happened next. What *had* to happen next. It had gone past being a choice, or something she asked for. Now it just felt inevitable, as if she couldn't pull away even if she wanted to.

And she *really* didn't want to.

'Happy New Year, Rachel,' Damon whispered back, and ducked his head just a little lower...

His lips against hers felt like heat and sex and they set New Year fireworks off behind her eyes—as though the sensation of kissing Damon Hunter after all these years might actually stun and blind her.

She could have kissed him for ever. Might have, if a production assistant in a sparkly dress hadn't elbowed her sharply and hissed, 'You're supposed to be singing!'

Sure enough, as she pulled back, Rachel realised that the rest of the guests were linking arms and bellowing out 'Auld Lang Syne', with varying levels of fidelity to the lyrics.

Damon rubbed the back of his neck with the hand that had, just moments ago, been holding her tightly against him. 'We should probably...'

'Right. Yes. Come on.' She darted back into the ring of people, linking arms with strangers who were suddenly far less scary than the one man she knew in the room, and hoping Damon took the hint to find some other people to sing with.

And then, when she was sure he wasn't looking, she ducked out of the circle, and headed for the door before anyone could stop her.

It wasn't midnight. It wasn't a new year or a fresh start, and she was still the same old Rachel Charles. Even if, just for a moment, she'd felt like someone else entirely.

# CHAPTER FOUR

WHERE HAD SHE GONE? Damon scanned the room, taking in all the tipsy partygoers still hugging and dancing now the midnight celebrations were over. The band was playing again—something upbeat, a tune that wouldn't have allowed him to hold Rachel so tantalisingly close against him.

If he could find her.

He vaguely remembered from the briefing before they started filming that there would be another few songs, then the host would wrap it up for the night, and welcome everyone into a brand-new year. Would Rachel come back for that last planned shot of them all clapping as the camera swooped up and away? He suspected not.

He'd kissed her. After spending the whole evening reminding himself that Rachel Charles, his sister's best friend, was categorically one of the few women of his acquaintance who had never given him any hint of romantic interest, he'd kissed her anyway. Which made him, officially, the worst sort of person.

Except...the way she'd clenched her fist around his jacket. Had that been nerves or something more? The way she'd fitted into his arms, the way she'd curled against him as they'd danced, her cheek against his chest...had he really been the only one whose heart had beat double fast at the sensation?

And *she* had stretched up towards him as the clock chimes rang out midnight, hadn't she? Had he really imagined all of that?

He sighed. Probably, yes.

It was because she'd been talking about That Night. That one night in his life when he'd felt understood. Open. Close enough to another person for them to see who he really was inside. For her he imagined it was a funny anecdote—the tale of them searching Oxford for Celeste only to find her asleep in the library the following morning, her phone on silent as always.

But for him, it had been a crossroads. Oh, he hadn't realised it at the time, of course; he'd been eighteen, drunk and scared for his sister. He hadn't realised anything much at the time. But afterwards—the next day, the next visit, whenever he saw Rachel again—he'd started to understand.

He'd pulled away from the closeness and the connection between them that night because it had scared him. He'd known himself well enough to realise that he didn't want the kind of expectation that came with a connection like that. Rachel wasn't like the usual girls he spent time with; she saw deeper than they did, and that meant something. He wouldn't be able to sleep with her then leave her behind.

So he'd put her firmly back in the box labelled 'Celeste's best friend' and kept her there. Until she mentioned that night and…

And trying to justify his actions to himself didn't make things any better. He'd kissed her, and she'd run away from him. That was all the information he needed.

She'd probably been planning on a quick peck on the cheek or something, just for the cameras. And, in truth, he'd not exactly been planning anything more than that himself. But as she'd swayed closer, something inside him had changed. Her scent in his lungs, his hand at her back, her breasts pressed against him…all he'd been able to think about was kissing her.

Celeste would tell him that this was where all his problems always started: with the inability to pass up an opportunity to charm and seduce.

He sank onto a bar stool at one of the high cocktail tables, and watched the party continue without him, and without Rachel. Everyone else seemed to be enjoying themselves, at least.

He should go and find Celeste. She *had* to have finished filming by now, right? It was— he glanced at the large clock, remembered its fakeness, and checked his watch instead—gone nine-thirty. They'd been at it for hours for a thirty-minute show, and they'd already lost half their audience.

As the band finished up their final song, Damon let himself silently out of the side door and hoped no one spotted him leaving.

He found Celeste stomping out of the green room, back in her usual black clothes but still with her hair and make-up TV-perfect. The scowl on her face wasn't, though.

'Where on earth did you go? And where's Rachel?'

'We got dragged in to film some New Year party show. They didn't have enough partygo-ers because of some issue on the Tube, and your filming had already gone longer than it was sup-posed to anyway.' The poor warm-up guy, the co-median who had to entertain the audience while they were waiting or between takes, must have more than earned his money that night.

Celeste rolled her eyes as she pushed past him to continue stomping down the corridor. 'Only because *that man* kept getting things wrong.'

Damon hid a smile. 'In fairness, Theo Mont-gomery was only reading out the answers on the cards.'

'Because he's not bright enough to actually know anything himself,' Celeste shot back over her shoulder. Then she winced, which was not an expression Damon was used to seeing from her. Neither was the slight tinge of pink that coloured her cheeks.

Eyebrows raised, he turned around to see what had caught her attention and found Theo Montgomery emerging from a room behind him into the corridor. From his raised eyebrows, he'd clearly heard everything Celeste had said.

Damon stepped towards him, hand out for Theo to shake, which he did.

'Mr Montgomery. I'm Damon Hunter, Celeste's brother—we met earlier? I just wanted to take this opportunity to apologise for my sister.'

'No need,' Theo said. 'Trust me, I've heard worse. You stayed for the whole filming?' He sounded amazed at the prospect.

Damon shook his head. 'No, I just follow my sister around to make the necessary apologies. And now that's done, I'm heading home.'

'Where's Rachel?' Celeste asked again, obviously ignoring Theo. 'I said we'd give her a lift home.'

'She, uh…she left early,' Damon said. It was the truth, after all, but apparently he couldn't avoid sounding guilty as he said it.

Celeste's eyes narrowed. 'What did you do?'

'What makes you think I did anything?' He

turned to Theo. 'Does it make you feel any better that she treats *everyone* this way?'

'A little,' Theo admitted.

'You always do something,' Celeste replied. 'Let me guess, you were flirting with some other woman at the bar and leaving her all on her own?'

'I can promise you that absolutely was not the case. I was attentive, friendly, we even danced together.' *And then I kissed her and she ran away.* Which made him feel sleazy and awful—not least because he was still reliving that kiss in his head. The way she had felt against him, how sweet her lips had been…

'Rachel *danced*?' Celeste asked, astonishment in her voice. 'I have never once, in ten full years, seen my best friend dance. There is something else going on here, and you are going to tell me all about it on the way home. Come on, let's get to the car.' Then, belatedly, she turned to Theo. 'Thank you for having me on your show, Mr Montgomery. I'm very sorry that the question team screwed up so many of your answer cards.'

Then she spun around and stalked down the corridor, obviously expecting Damon to chase after her. He sighed, and turned back to Theo.

'Once again, apologies for my sister's attempt at an apology.'

But Theo, surprisingly, was smiling. 'No need.

She certainly livened up the experience—and I'm pretty sure our researchers will be stepping up their game if we ever have her on again.'

'I think *if* is the important word in that sentence.'

Theo laughed. 'You might be right. Goodnight.'

''Night.' Damon turned and headed after Celeste, steeling himself for the grilling he was about to get in the car. Maybe he should have just lied and told her he'd been flirting with another woman. He had a feeling that would have gone down much better with Celeste than the truth.

He practised telling her what had happened in his head.

*I kissed your best friend.*

Yeah, no. That wasn't going to go down any better with Celeste than it had with Rachel.

He sighed. Nothing about this evening had turned out how he'd expected. And yet, as he remembered dancing with Rachel…he couldn't honestly say he wanted to change any of it.

Rachel could hear the Christmas carols playing on the shop floor, along with the chaos of a department store at the beginning of December as customers fought to find the best presents, most flattering party outfits and, of course, the best seasonal deals. In her tiny office—okay, fine, converted cupboard—at the far end of the homewares floor, she was mostly protected from the fuss and bother outside. She didn't have a shift on the tills until tomorrow, the window displays were all perfect, and that meant she could get on with designing, writing and scheduling Hartbury & Sons' seasonal messages.

When she'd brainstormed her seasonal campaigns back in August, she'd been excited to get started. But, as so often happened, the everyday requirements of her job and her family had taken over, and now here she was at the start of December and she still had most of her Christmas posts still to write.

Hannah and the store's board of directors were an old-fashioned bunch when it came to marketing. When it came to most things, actually. A couple of half-page adverts in relevant newspapers once a season and they thought they were done. After all, as Hannah always said, Hartbury's was an institution. They didn't *need* to advertise.

Except, as Rachel had tried to explain to them so many times before, the world was changing. Yes, people might have *heard* of Hartbury's, but unless they gave them a reason to visit, unless they showed them why they were still relevant to a new generation of shoppers, getting new people through the doors was only going to get harder. She'd eventually talked them into hiring a company to set up and manage the online store, but only because they could see that would give them actual sales from people living in corners of the world too far away to just pop down to Hartbury's—first she'd had to remind them that such places, outside London, actually existed but she'd got there.

Hiring an online marketing team, or even a social media manager, though, that was a step too far. Which meant it fell to Rachel to bring the store into the twenty-first century, whether she liked it or not.

She looked at the new images she'd created for her social media campaign, and wondered if they were just a little...blah. She'd gone for classic festive images, the sort that Hartbury's always used in their adverts, or around the store, but now she was thinking that maybe she could do something a little more...personal. Maybe she'd go and take some new photos of her finished window displays, and use those. Hannah tolerated the window displays because they delighted the kids, which meant the parents were happier while shopping, but Rachel knew she'd personally prefer something more traditionally Christmas. She'd probably hate the idea that Rachel's displays were representing the store online, but since Hannah didn't use social media, she might never notice.

And her window displays were good. Even Damon said so—

'Dammit!' Rachel picked up her notebook and made another tally mark, then checked her watch. Five minutes that time. She'd gone a whole five minutes without thinking about Damon Hunter, and That Kiss. That might be an actual record, the longest she'd managed since she ran out of the studio on Tuesday night.

Now it was Thursday, and she was still spending more time thinking about him than anything else. Not a great sign.

Celeste had called the next day to apologise for whatever her brother had done to offend or annoy her, but Rachel had told her it was nothing. In fact, she'd lied and said she'd just had a headache.

She could tell from the sceptical silence on the other end of the line that Celeste hadn't believed her, but it was clear that Damon hadn't told her what had happened either, and Rachel was determined she wasn't going to spill.

She'd been the besotted girl before, the one who thought a guy truly liked her only to find out it was all a joke—or at least, that she wasn't important enough to be serious about. In fact, she'd been that girl *twice*. Once in high school, when she figured it was normal to be that naive. But the second time had been only last summer, with Tobias, and that time Rachel really should have known better.

This time, she *did* know better. Damon had been in her life for a decade and at no point had he given her even a *hint* that he saw her as anything other than his big sister's best friend. He wasn't cruel enough to pretend to like her for a bet, or to laugh off any relationship between them as a joke as Gretchen's friend Tobias ultimately had, but she also wasn't going to let herself believe it was anything more than a spur-of-the-moment impulse. A New Year's Eve kiss in the moment and then forgotten about.

By him anyway.

Forcing herself to refocus, Rachel turned back to her social media work—until a knock on the door broke her concentration again.

'Rach?' Her dad stuck his head around the door. She looked up and scanned his expression, his complexion, looking for signs of how he was feeling, whether the medicine was working. As ever, there were no firm answers. 'Ah good, I've found you. Um…can I come in?'

'You can try.' Rachel looked around at her tiny cupboard office, and wondered exactly where her dad thought he was going to stand. By the time the desk, chair and precariously balanced book-shelf were accounted for, there wasn't really any floor space left.

He settled for hovering in the open doorway, giving Rachel a view past him of the shop floor and all the Christmas shoppers she was trying to avoid.

'Am I needed on the shop floor?' she asked, when her father stayed silent.

He shook his head. 'No, no. Just…your step-mother thought you'd been a little bit down the last couple of days. She thought you might be worrying about what to wear for the Christmas party.'

'I'm not—' Rachel started, but her father kept talking over her, desperate as ever to make every-thing all right again without ever understanding what the real problem was.

'So we bought you this!' He pulled a pine green and red tartan monstrosity out of the bag in his hands and held it up for her to appreciate.

She didn't know how they'd managed it, but her dad and Hannah had found a dress she hated even more than any of the ones her stepsisters had made her try on the other day. This one would cover her from neck to mid-calf, with the green and red tartan pattern swamping her completely. The fabric looked stiff and uncomfortable. And the whole thing was capped off with a bright red satin bow, as a five-year-old might wear.

'Isn't it lovely?' Her father looked down at the dress lovingly. She imagined he was seeing her as a little girl again, wearing it. Or maybe the heart medication he was on had affected his sartorial taste somehow. 'Hannah has such exquisite taste, and I know you'll be grateful she was thinking of you.'

There was just the edge of desperate hope in his words, the same tone she'd been hearing ever since her father remarried two years after her mother died. The subtle reminder that he was doing all this for her, really. That he wanted her to be happy. That he needed them all to be a family.

Her father was genuinely fond of Hannah, loved her even. But Rachel had often wondered if he'd have remarried so quickly if it hadn't been for her. He'd been falling apart after his wife's death, and all anyone seemed to say was that a teenage girl needed a mother, a family.

So he'd found Hannah, and Rachel had spent the last fourteen years not fitting in with the family he'd chosen for them. To start with, because she hadn't been ready to leave the memory of her mother behind. She'd been awkward, difficult—really, she'd been fourteen, that was all. Gretchen and Maisie were both younger, and their parents had been divorced for years. Rachel and her dad had moved into their family home, but otherwise nothing had really changed for them.

But for Rachel, *everything* had changed. And most days, she still lived with the fallout.

*Wait for Dad's test results. If they're clear, I'll talk to him about finding my own place to live. One step at a time.*

Rachel swallowed her true feelings about the tartan monstrosity, and tried not to think about the cranberry-red wrap dress with the forest animal pattern she'd worn to the party the other night. The dress Damon had bought her, because it made him think of her.

Her family looked at her and thought, *Cover her up with tartan*, or *Hide her away in the corner*, or even *Embarrass the hell out of her.*

Damon looked at her and thought she deserved a dress she loved, one that felt like the way she saw *herself.*

Surely that had to mean something, didn't it?

Her father was still waiting for her verdict on the dress. And she'd promised herself—and Hannah—that she'd try to keep the peace, try not to be difficult, while his health was so delicate.

'It's very festive,' she said, carefully picking her way around the truth. 'It was so kind of Hannah to think of me like that.'

Her dad's face relaxed into a smile. 'I knew you'd like it! I'll take it home for you and hang it in your room. Save it getting creased in here.' He glanced around her office again with a frown. 'And you know, now you mention it, it is very busy on the shop floor today. I'm sure Hannah would appreciate it if you lent a hand.'

'I'll be right there,' Rachel promised, trying hard not to sigh. Apparently her social media campaign would have to wait. Again.

Closing down her laptop, she added another tally to her chart—thinking about the dress definitely counted as thinking about Damon—and prepared to head out to work. But as she grabbed her phone, she saw she had a new message.

From Damon.

What are you doing this afternoon?

He'd tried to forget that kiss, really he had. Tried to push aside whatever impulse had led him to kiss his sister's best friend. Tried to forget how spending time with her again had sent him back to that other night they'd spent talking, and how the connection between them had scared eighteen-year-old him so much he'd run in the opposite direction. To remind himself, hourly if necessary, that she was an old family friend who had never given him a *hint* of interest—and had actually run away from him when he'd showed some.

He'd tried.

He'd failed.

As he stood in the middle of his latest business project, Damon tried to convince himself that his interest in Rachel Charles was actually totally professional—the same way he'd convinced himself, nine years ago, that their connection was simply shared concern for the missing Celeste.

Fake midnight kiss aside, what they'd mostly talked about was her work—most especially, her window displays. He was genuinely interested in the tableaus she put together, and he had a legitimate reason to contact her about them. Nothing to do with the kiss.

The question was, if he called her about work would she answer?

There was only one way to find out, he supposed. His phone in his hand, his fingers hovered over the keyboard for a moment, then he dashed out a text and put his phone back in his pocket.

What are you doing this afternoon?

Neutral, giving her an easy out, definitely more of a friendly tone than anything else, right? So why was his heart pounding waiting for her answer?

This was about work. He had to remember that.

As if the universe figured he might need some help doing so, the gate at the far end of the Cressingham Arcade creaked open and his client, Lady Cressingham herself, strode in.

Lady Cressingham was, Damon had learned over the last week or two, quite simply a force of nature. Today, she was dressed in a rich plum-coloured wool coat with a fake fur collar, matching leather gloves and shiny black boots. Her hair was perfectly set despite the winter wind, and large diamonds glittered at her throat and earlobes.

Her eyes narrowed as she approached him, the heels of her boots clacking against the tiled floor of the arcade. 'So? Any progress to report?' she asked, her clipped upper-class tones as cold as the icy weather.

Damon raised an eyebrow, and glanced surreptitiously over his shoulder. Ah, that explained it. Old Mr Jenkins was watching them from his shop window, polishing cloth in his hands as he set out his jewellery display for the day. He was the biggest hold out to their whole plan, so Lady Cressingham always took care to be sharper, more professional, when he was watching.

In truth, their whole acquaintance had started at a party held in a top London art gallery, hosted by a mutual friend. Damon always made a point of talking to new people at events like that; just chatting with the same old crowd rarely threw up any new and interesting opportunities. When he'd spotted Lady Cressingham in her scarlet evening gown and silver wrap he'd just known she would have an interesting story—and he'd been right.

He'd never asked her age, and Wikipedia had been strangely coy on the subject, but he guessed she had to be in her sixties, if not her seventies. She'd been married to Lord Cressingham for as long as anyone could remember; the rumours were that he'd been cheating on her since their wedding day. Not just rumours, actually. Lady Cressingham had been quite open on the subject the night they'd met.

'We have an arrangement of sorts, I suppose,' she'd told Damon. 'I ignore the fact that he's a philandering son of a you-know-what who can't keep his trousers fastened, and he lets me spend his family fortune on causes that appeal to me, and to speculate on projects that have the potential to make me a lot of money, while also helping others.'

She was a jack of all trades when it came to businesses, just like himself, it turned out. Maybe that was what had drawn them together in the first place. All he knew was that a month after that party, she'd called him up out of the blue with a proposition.

'Come and run my latest project for me. I need someone with an entrepreneurial eye.'

Damon had been between projects and he'd been intrigued. And so he'd said yes.

Which was how he came to be standing in the middle of the shabby, slightly crumbling Cressingham Arcade, being glared at by an antisocial jeweller, imagining what magic Rachel could work with the window displays in this place.

Lady Cressingham was still waiting for a project update, though.

'I do have some new progress, and some new ideas to talk through with you.' His phone buzzed in his pocket. 'Excuse me one second.'

Pulling it out, he checked the screen and saw the one-word answer from Rachel.

Yes.

'In fact,' he went on, stashing his phone away again, 'if you have time for afternoon tea today, there's someone I'd like you to meet. Someone who might be the key to turning this place into everything you've been dreaming of.'

Lady Cressingham raised a sceptical eyebrow, but nodded all the same. 'Book us a table at the Ritz at three. If nothing else, I want to make the aquaintance of the woman whose text message just put that smile on your face.'

# CHAPTER FIVE

Rachel had lived in London her whole life and never been for afternoon tea at the Ritz. She supposed most people hadn't, really. It wasn't exactly an everyday occurrence. Unless you were Lady Cressingham, apparently, who seemed to know all the waiters by their first names.

She'd assumed, when Damon had told her to meet him at Piccadilly Circus, that it would just be the two of them. And she definitely hadn't imagined he'd be taking her to the Ritz. If she had, she might have worn something slightly more suitable for the occasion. Or not, because actually, now she thought about it, she wasn't sure she even owned anything suitable for taking afternoon tea with a member of the aristocracy at one of London's most famous hotels.

Maybe the dress Damon had bought her. Except she wasn't allowing herself to think about that dress, or what had happened last time she wore it.

Because this wasn't a date, or even a friendly catch-up. Or, as she'd sort of assumed, Damon's attempt to let her down gently. Last time she'd thought she was close to Damon, even without a kiss to mark the occasion, he'd made it obvious—in a kind way—that it was just a one-off. The next time he'd visited, she'd been very clearly relegated back to 'Celeste's friend,' rather than a friend of his in her own right. And she'd stayed that way until he'd kissed her two days ago.

Of course he'd want to set the record straight again. The thought had occurred to her as soon as she'd seen his text. Damon, despite his play-boy reputation, was always scrupulously honest with his flings—she knew that from Celeste. He never led them on, and always made it clear up front how much—or how little—he was willing to give.

As Celeste put it, *'I understand him not wanting to get into a romantic tangle. They can be so messy if you aren't both straight upfront about what you're entering into, or if one of you has higher expectations than the other.'*

She made it sound more like a business arrangement than a love affair, Rachel thought, though she hadn't said that.

*'But Damon doesn't even have those discussions with his girlfriends. He just tells them straight not to expect anything past one night. Anything extra is just a bonus.'*

But he hadn't had a chance to tell Rachel that, so she figured he was worrying she was reading more into that midnight kiss than was really there. All the way to Piccadilly on the Tube she'd been planning the most casual way to let him know that she had absolutely no expectations of him; she knew better than that.

Except it seemed that wasn't why he'd invited her at all.

'How are you finding the cucumber sandwiches, dear?' Lady Cressingham asked her, across the table. Between them, sitting at the end of the loaded table, Damon sat devouring a scone slathered in jam and cream, apparently oblivious to the many, many questions Rachel had about this whole gathering.

'They're delicious.' She put her half-nibbled sandwich down on her plate. 'In fact, this whole spread is incredible. I'm just...wondering, well... I mean, I just wasn't sure...'

'Why Damon invited you to tea?' Lady Cressingham finished for her, shaking her head. 'Damon, dear, I was led to understand that you were much smoother with the ladies than this.'

Rachel's eyes widened and she sat bolt upright, ready to correct the obvious mistaken assumption. 'Oh, no, Damon and I...we're old friends, that's all, really.'

Lady Cressingham looked unconvinced, but waved away Rachel's protests all the same. 'I'm not sure our Damon *has* old friends, only new ones. But in this case, I believe he's brought you here for a business proposal, rather than a personal one.' She shot an unreadable look along the table at Damon. 'At least, that's what he seems to believe.'

Confused, Rachel turned to Damon too. 'A business proposal?' How could she possibly be of use to him with one of those? She didn't even really know what his business *was*.

'Lady Cressingham has hired me to manage her latest project for her,' Damon explained. But before he could say any more, Lady Cressingham took over.

'The Cressingham Arcade,' she explained. 'It's not exactly in the most fashionable area of the city, but it's respectable enough, and it's been languishing in my husband's property portfolio for far too long. I decided it was time to make proper use of it for a change.'

'A shopping arcade?' Rachel asked, still baffled as to what her part was going to be in this.

'A small one. Set back from a reasonably busy shopping street, but currently woefully ignored by passing shoppers.' Lady Cressingham shook her head at her bite-sized lemon cake. 'Such a waste. And of course my husband has completely forgotten that he even owned it.'

How rich did a person have to be to forget that they owned a shopping arcade? Rachel could hardly imagine. She gazed around at the opulent surroundings of the Ritz restaurant and its patrons. Perhaps for a person who judged tea there as an everyday occurrence, property ownership became just as ordinary.

'It has eight shops,' Damon went on, ticking them off on his fingers as he went. 'At present, three are unoccupied, two are recently let and three have long-standing occupants. So right now there's a jeweller's, a florist's, a stationer's, a chocolate shop and a wedding dress boutique.'

'It sounds…lovely?' Rachel said, still confused as to her part in this.

'It could be,' Lady Cressingham said, dryly. 'It needs a lot of TLC, but Damon has the decorators and builders coming in for that. It needs some more tenants too, but I've got my feelers out. I only want a certain sort of business in my arcade.'

Rachel nodded. Clearly the aristocracy had standards about who they rented to. She shouldn't be surprised about that.

But Damon shot a fond smile at the older lady. 'You're giving Rachel the idea you're elitist, you know.'

Lady Cressingham drew herself up to her full seated height. Which, since her posture had been impeccable since they'd sat down, was quite an achievement. 'Well, I do have very strict criteria.'

Damon rolled his eyes. 'What she means is that

she will only rent the unoccupied shops to people, usually women, looking for a fresh start in life.'

That...wasn't what Rachel had expected at all. She gave the aristocrat across the table a surprised look, which Lady Cressingham politely pretended not to see as she poured herself another cup of Assam tea.

'People need a little help sometimes, when they're starting over,' she said, stirring her cup. 'And I'm in a position to give them that. That's all.'

But she didn't have to, Rachel knew. Plenty of people had all the money in the world and only used it to make more. And while she was sure that Lady Cressingham intended for the arcade to become a profitable business, that didn't change the fact that she wanted to do some good with it too.

Rachel still couldn't see exactly where she fitted into all this. But suddenly, she desperately wanted to know.

*This* could be the first step she'd been looking for, without even knowing it. She'd been so focussed on following her plodding plan—get the test results, make sure Dad was okay, move out, start thinking about new jobs—and Damon, in his usual chaotic style, had come in and ripped up the whole strategy.

But he was giving her an opportunity she hadn't even envisioned. The chance to do something that might matter to people, just a bit. That was what she needed, and she hadn't even realised it until now.

Plus, working on a new project might distract her from thinking about that kiss. That was just an added bonus.

Placing her forearms on the table, she leant forward. 'Okay. How can I help?'

Damon saw the moment when Rachel went from wanting to run away from this strange tea party to actively wanting to help. He smiled to himself as Lady Cressingham pushed the plate of scones towards her. She approved of Rachel, he could tell. He wasn't sure why that was important to him, but apparently it was.

More crucially, Rachel approved of the Cressingham Arcade project. And that really did matter to him.

He wanted to talk to her about the other night— *about that kiss*, his brain supplied, unhelpfully— but there hadn't been time between meeting her off the Tube, and meeting Lady Cressingham at the Ritz. And since he still wasn't entirely sure what he wanted to say about it, beyond apologising if he'd got the wrong message, he hadn't exactly pushed the point. Also, that uneasy feeling of being with someone who saw too deep inside him, the way she had years ago, seemed to be back and he didn't like it any more now than he had then. He needed to re-establish some boundaries, and talking about kissing definitely wasn't going to achieve that.

The personal could wait. They had business to discuss first.

'Like Lady Cressingham said, the whole place is having a bit of a do-over. We're putting in new tiles for the floors, touching up all the paintwork, having new signs painted, the works. But all that means we're not going to be able to open properly to the public until later in the month—'

'Right before Christmas,' Rachel said, grasping the problem immediately. She worried her lower lip between her teeth, in a way Damon tried to convince himself he didn't find adorable. The line between her eyebrows when she was concentrating was pretty cute too.

*Focus, Damon.*

'Exactly,' he said. 'Which means we're missing a lot of the prime Christmas shopping time.' Hell, it was already the third of December. They'd missed a lot of it already, but that couldn't be helped. And it wasn't as if the arcade was doing a roaring trade before they started, however much Mr Jenkins might be complaining now about the disruption.

'You need to get people talking about the arcade before it even opens,' Rachel said, thinking aloud. 'You want a buzz about the place, so people are excited to visit that first day, maybe even hold off on some of their shopping until you open.' Her eyes widened as she seemed to realise that she was telling Lady Cressingham what to do. 'I mean, that's what I'd suggest. Or what I'd do. But I'm sure you both know better than I do about these things.'

Lady Cressingham selected a miniature Victoria sponge from the cake stand. 'Actually, dear, I don't think we do. That's why Damon brought you in. So, tell me: what else would you do to make my arcade the only place anyone wants to shop this Christmas?'

Rachel hesitated. Watching her closely—not least because she was nibbling her bottom lip again and he just couldn't look away—he tried to figure out what was stopping her. She knew this stuff; he'd checked out the social media accounts for Hartbury's, and as far as he could see they were head and shoulders above what most stores were doing. People really engaged with her posts about the window displays, more than anything. Her stepmother must be thrilled at all the extra attention she was bringing in…

Her stepmother. Hartbury's. Of course.

'The arcade would be a completely different sort of business to Hartbury's,' he said, quickly. 'Different clientele too. I mean, the stores there sell personalised, one-off sort of items most of the time. Lots of handmade things too. Nothing like your stepmother's store.'

Lady Cressingham caught onto the problem promptly. 'Absolutely! We'd never ask you to undermine your family business, of course not. And Hartbury's has a very fine reputation. But I do not believe that the products sold would truly be commensurate with those sold in the Cressingham Arcade.'

Rachel gave a slow nod. 'You're right, I suppose.'

'And you did tell me the other night that you'd like to go freelance one day, doing social media and marketing for other companies,' Daman added, persuasively, he hoped. 'This could be your first step. Help you start building your portfolio.'

'Of course, we'd pay you fairly as well,' Lady Cressingham put it. 'I'm aware that we're asking a lot here, but from what Damon has told me—and showed me, online—I think you're the perfect person for this job.'

Damon hid a smile. Even Lady Cressingham had been beyond charmed by the photos of Rachel's window displays. She'd seen instantly what he was suggesting.

'We need to bring the whole arcade together,' Damon explained, remembering that reaction. 'At the moment, they're more of a mishmash of enterprises. We need to somehow make it feel cohesive, like they belong together.'

'Like each shop is part of the bigger whole...' Rachel mused. 'You're thinking about the window displays?' she guessed.

Damon grinned. 'Of course! Between your incredible displays *and* your social media skills, plus my more traditional and modest abilities, I think we can have half of London begging to visit the Cressingham Arcade by the time we open.'

'Only half?' Lady Cressingham asked, over the rim of her teacup. 'Dear boy, I don't think you're aiming high enough.'

By the time crumbs and tealeaves were all that was left of their afternoon tea, Rachel had worked her way through fear, doubt, uncertainty and at least some of her imposter-syndrome issues, and arrived at excitement. Despite all the courses she'd taken, all the work she'd put in at Hartbury's, a part of her, deep down, had never really believed she'd be able to do this sort of thing for a real job, outside the family business.

Today, Damon had shown her that she could.

She was excited by this project, by the chance to put into practice all the ideas she'd been dreaming up that she knew her stepmother would never let her use. Excited to work towards Lady Cressingham's dream of a shopping arcade that could be beautiful, a shopping destination, a helping hand for people changing their lives *and* a viable business, all at the same time.

Excited, although she refused to admit it, even to herself, to work with Damon too.

They'd hashed out a plan between them of all the work there was to do. Quite when she was going to fit it all in, between her shifts at the department store, work on Hartbury's social media and her own Christmas preparations, Rachel wasn't entirely sure. But she *would*. Because this mattered to her.

She couldn't remember the last time something other than her father had really, really mattered to her like this.

Maybe this was what had been missing for so long. Maybe *this* was the push she needed to change her life.

'So,' Damon said as Lady Cressingham paid the bill. 'Do you want to come and see the arcade now?'

His smile was wicked, as if he were inviting her up to see his etchings. Maybe he was, in a way. This project, this opportunity, was the perfect way into her heart—or at least into her pants. Making her feel competent, talented even, and wanted. It didn't take much, did it?

'Yes. Definitely.'

But Damon hadn't even mentioned the kiss.

Probably because he hadn't thought of it since it happened—while it had consumed her every waking moment.

She wasn't the kind of girl that guys like Damon wanted. Her experience with Tobias should have taught her that.

Rachel shook away her thoughts as she reached for her bag and coat. This was about more than a kiss, or an attraction anyway. This was a professional opportunity she wanted to take full advantage of.

The chance to figure out her own path in life, not just the one her family expected her to walk.

This was work. Not pleasure.

But as she moved to put her coat on, Damon took it from her and held it out for her, like a proper, old-fashioned gentleman. Swallowing, she smiled her thanks and turned to ease her arms into the sleeves. Damon assisted, lifting the coat over her shoulders and smoothing it down over her arms.

Rachel froze at the close contact. She could almost imagine he was about to wrap her up in his embrace. To hold her as close as he had when they'd danced.

For a long moment, he remained near enough that she could catch hints of his cologne, could almost feel his breath against her cheek. For that long moment, hope blossomed in her chest...

And then he stepped away.

'Come on, you two,' Lady Cressingham said, either impatience or amusement colouring her voice, Rachel wasn't entirely sure which. Maybe it was both. She didn't seem like the sort of woman to waste precious minutes only having one emotion at a time. 'I've had the car brought round.'

The Cressingham Arcade was everything Rachel had hoped it would be.

From the elegantly curving iron gates to the vintage tiled floor between the shop fronts—which Damon assured her they'd be restoring rather than replacing—it screamed refined elegance, much like Lady Cressingham herself. The shop names were a mishmash of different styles, but Damon showed her the prototype for the new ones. Each shop face would have a matching wooden sign painted in the colours taken from the floor tiles—dark forest greens, creams, duck-egg blues and hints of blush pink—with the name of the shop in a scrolling vintage font.

Between each shop rose sleek columns, tiled to match the floor, until they reached the ceiling and met as carved stone overhead, almost like a cathedral. Rachel tilted her head as far back as it would go, and imagined fairy lights illuminating every shadow up there.

And then there were the windows. The beautiful, deep bay windows that jutted out from every storefront into the passageway that formed the arcade, each with a wooden display area inside just *begging* to be decorated. Standing there, Rachel felt a million ideas start to swirl inside her brain, and knew she'd never be short of ways to decorate or promote this magical place.

'What do you think?' Damon asked, his voice suddenly very close as he rested his chin on her shoulder to stare into the window with her.

'It's magical,' she whispered, and felt him smile.

'This is what your windows reminded me of. This place. And I just knew I had to get you involved over here, to make the arcade everything it can be.'

Warmth flooded through her at his words. Damon Hunter thought *she* was a match for this wonderful, secret place. And suddenly, she could almost believe it too.

Damon stepped away. 'Come on. I want to introduce you to some of the shopkeepers here.'

The next half an hour was a whirl of new people, more than Rachel thought she'd met in one go since university. Lady Cressingham was deep in conversation with an older gentleman at the end of the arcade so Damon started the introductions at the nearest occupied shop—a florist called Belinda, with incredible wreaths of ivy, holly, berries and such sitting on tables out front.

'Technically we're still open,' Belinda explained. 'Although you wouldn't know it from all the cones and boards out front. But I had a wreath-making class booked for today and I wasn't going to cancel it just because this one wants to spruce the place up a bit.' She jerked her head towards Damon as she said 'this one', and he rolled his eyes in response. But they were both smiling, so Rachel assumed everyone was okay with what he had planned for the place, despite the disruption.

'The wreaths are beautiful,' she said to Belinda, who beamed proudly. 'They'd be wonderful in a window display…' She could envisage it already: a forest scene, with a wreath on every tree, lights throughout, Christmas tubs and pot plants at the base of the trees…

'Belinda always keeps the window clear,' the florist's assistant, Ursula, said as she tidied away the wreath-making supplies. 'She likes to be able to see out.'

'Oh. Right.' Rachel shot a quick glance at Damon who shrugged, as if to say, *This is what I'm dealing with. Why do you think I need you?*

Deciding to try a different tack, Rachel asked, 'It looks like the wreath-making workshop was a great success. Did you promote it on social media?'

'Oh, these are just the wreaths I made to show

people what's possible,' Belinda explained. 'The four people we had in took their wreaths home with them, of course.'

'I did put the dates up on our new Facebook page,' Ursula added. 'But I don't think many people saw it. You know how it is.' She shrugged, and went back to clearing up.

Rachel quickly learned that it was the same story throughout the arcade. People were focussed on their shops, on keeping their heads above water. They didn't have time to learn the ins and outs of social media algorithms or how to build their fan base online.

That was what they needed her for.

As Damon led her out of the florist's, they discovered that most of the other shopkeepers had come out to meet her too. Rachel smiled politely, and tried hard to affix names to faces and shops in her brain, knowing that the odds of her remembering them all were slim. She'd have to get Damon to write them all down for her later. He was the people person, after all, not her.

And that had never been more evident than here. With every new arrival Damon was able to introduce them without hesitation, and tell her the basics of their work there. But more than that, he interacted with each person on a level that showed he knew their circumstances, their opinions, and remembered everything they'd ever said to him.

Rachel could barely remember her own computer password most days. Or the names of some of her seasonal co-workers. She didn't *do* people, not the way Damon did.

And with every introduction, he managed to lead the conversation around to exactly where she needed it.

'Jasmine's bridal boutique is one of the newest shops in the arcade, isn't it, Jasmine?' he said, motioning over a petite blonde woman in a pastel-pink jumper. 'She's keen to convince London's brides that she's got the perfect dress for them—which means getting the message out to the world that *her* boutique has the unique dresses that others just don't.'

'We only stock smaller designers,' Jasmine explained. 'And I design bespoke gowns for brides too.'

'So this is where to come if you want a wedding dress that doesn't look like everyone else's?'

'Exactly!' Jasmine said, beaming.

Rachel filed that information away in the part of her brain that was already planning everything she could do for the shopping arcade. Information, she could remember. It was people she struggled with.

But the people were what was going to make Cressingham Arcade special, she could feel it.

# CHAPTER SIX

BY THE TIME Damon had finished introducing Rachel to all the occupants of the Cressingham Arcade—right down to the ornery Mr Jenkins, who grumbled through the whole meeting about not agreeing with all this modern stuff—the sun had long gone down. The shops were all shut up and the shopkeepers departed for home. Even Lady Cressingham had left. Apart from a few sad-looking fairy lights outside the florist's shop, the arcade was almost in darkness, the glow of the moon and the streetlights outside only just penetrating the gloom.

'I should probably get going,' Rachel said, glancing at the backlit screen of her phone and checking the time. 'It's getting late.'

He should let her go, Damon knew. She was right, it *was* late. And it wasn't as if he didn't have more work to do. And yet…

'Wait here a moment.' Dashing back into the small office at the far end of the arcade, Damon pulled out two torches from the well-stocked emergency drawer, then shut and locked the office behind him.

'We couldn't just turn some lights on?' Rachel asked as he handed her the torch.

He grinned. 'It's more fun this way.'

The arcade looked so different at night, something he'd discovered over late nights working in the office, planning out the renovations and scheduling the work. Without the modern lighting, and with the streets outside quietening, it was almost as if they'd travelled back in time—back two hundred years or more, to when the arcade was first built.

'So where are we going?' Rachel asked, turning on her torch and shining it around the tiled floors.

'We're staying right here,' Damon explained. 'I want to show you the other side of the arcade. Not the everyday shopping one that everyone sees. The magical, after-hours one.'

'I'd like to see that.' Even in the pale torchlight, her smile was unmissable. It warmed Damon's heart, despite the chill of the winter air. There was mischief in that smile, and a love of life that he had rarely ever seen from Rachel before.

*Apart from when I kissed her.*

He pushed down the memory. 'Come on, then.' Grabbing her hand, he led her to the far end of the arcade, to start his after-hours tour.

'Down here, we have one of my favourite details of the whole arcade,' he announced grandly.

Then he shone his torchlight on the spot in question, a bit of wall just above the floor.

Rachel crouched down to get a closer look, jumped back a little, then laughed—just as Damon had hoped she would.

'Someone painted a mouse and a mouse hole on the wall?' She stood up again, and he moved his light so he could see her face. She looked utterly charmed by the detail.

He nodded. 'Nobody knows when—could have been decades ago, to be honest, or possibly even when the place was built, although I suspect the paint would need to have been touched up from time to time.'

'But why would they do it?' she asked. 'I mean, is it vandalism or whimsy?'

'I figured it was like the mice in your window, actually,' Damon replied. 'A little surprise for those who look deeper. That's not the only one, either.'

'There are more?' Rachel's eyes were wide in the torchlight. 'Can we see them all?'

How could he refuse her when she looked so delighted at the prospect? 'Of course. Come this way, milady.'

They found four more mice at ground level and Rachel was so thrilled he probably could have stopped there. But he wanted to keep that smile on her face, that wonder in her eyes. She was falling for this arcade the same way he had. Well, maybe not quite the same way—he'd been more enamoured by the business potential first, then the people, then the whimsical discoveries he'd made as he'd explored the place. He could tell that Rachel had seen the potential this afternoon, talking with the shopkeepers, seen how much of a difference she could make here. This creature treasure hunt was only cementing that.

'Is that all of them?' she asked as he led her back to where they'd started.

'Not quite.' He was holding her hand again, Damon realised. When had that happened? Or had he never let it go? No, he must have done, because she'd moved away to trace the outlines of the mice they'd found right by the front gate. Which meant he'd reached out and taken her hand again—or she'd taken his.

It made sense, in the darkness. It was practical, that was all. But still, now he was aware of it, he couldn't ignore the tingling sensation her fingers, intertwined in his, gave him. Or how natural it felt.

He wasn't a hand-holding kind of guy, never had been. The women he tended to take out might hold onto his arm, more for balance or support in their uncomfortable shoes than anything else, he suspected. But they never held hands. That was too…intimate. Somehow more so than taking a woman home to bed.

But Rachel was holding his hand as if it was the most natural thing in the world. And weirdly, it felt as if it was.

'Where are we going?' she asked as he opened a door that was hidden between two tiled pillars, and painted to look like an extension of the walls.

'Up,' he replied, cryptically.

The curving metal staircase clanked under their feet, the sound echoing off the walls of the silent arcade. At the top, Damon fiddled with the latch on a second hidden door, pushed it open, then stepped back to let Rachel through first.

He could sense her nerves, her uncertainty of walking into the unknown, but he knew it would be worth it for her. Squeezing her hand, he let go, and she stepped out onto the small wrought-iron balcony. Shining the torch out beyond her, to the ceiling of the arcade, he waited.

'Oh!' Rachel gasped, and turned back to face him, her hand over her mouth and delight in her eyes. 'Look at them!' She grasped the metal rail of the balcony and leant out, just a little, her chin tilted upwards as she stared at the ceiling. 'How did I not see them from the ground?'

'They're hidden in the pattern.' Damon stepped closer behind her, looking upwards to take in the painted butterflies scattered around the ceiling.

'From the floor, it just looks like an attractively painted ceiling. But from here…'

'It comes to life,' she breathed, finishing his sentence for him. Above them, intricately decorated butterflies almost seemed to flutter around the archways and shadows of the arcade. 'It's like the houses in my window.'

'Exactly.' It was what had made him think of Rachel, of bringing her in. The moment he'd seen the tiny mice living their secret lives in her window displays, out of sight of the adults hurrying past, he'd known that she was meant to be here at the Cressingham Arcade, with the mice and the butterflies. And him.

She spun around suddenly, catching him by surprise, and he wrapped an arm around her waist instinctively, in case she lost her balance on the narrow balcony. She didn't, of course, but now she was pressed almost against him, so close he could feel the warmth of her breath against his neck as she looked up at him. Her eyes were luminous in the faint light from the torch he now held at the small of her back, and her lips were slightly parted. They looked soft and inviting and… He was thinking about kissing her. Again.

'Thank you for bringing me here,' Rachel whispered, and hearing the hoarseness in her voice he wondered if she was thinking about it too. If maybe he wasn't the only one remembering how it had felt that night on the dance floor, her mouth under his... 'For showing me this, I mean. It's very special.'

*So are you*, he thought, but didn't say it.

She was his sister's best friend. Celeste would never forgive him if he seduced Rachel, not even if she wanted to be seduced. Not when he had nothing to offer her beyond a few nights in bed together.

Rachel deserved more than that. He'd known that much since he'd first met her, and only had it cemented when he'd spent a whole night talking with her. Rachel was special. Anyone who could put up with Celeste as a best friend deserved a medal, at the very least. But more than that, she deserved love.

And Damon couldn't give her that. So...

'I thought you'd like it.' He stepped back, letting go of her waist. It seemed harder, this time, than it had when he was eighteen.

That night, he'd known that if he'd kissed her, she'd have fallen into his arms. But he'd also known that one night with her wouldn't have been enough—for either of them. And he didn't do more than one night. So he'd pulled away, just like now.

If she was disappointed, she didn't show it. Instead, she nodded vigorously. 'I do. Not just the hidden animals…the whole arcade. I can already see how magical it could be—*will* be, I hope.'

'So you'll help Lady Cressingham and me with the project?'

She met his gaze with her own excited one and something caught in his chest again as she answered. Something somewhere in the vicinity of his heart.

'I will.'

Rachel covered a yawn with her hand as she waited for the staff meeting to begin. There was still an hour before the department store opened, which meant it was far too early to be dealing with the crowds of staff pouring in, especially without coffee.

And especially given the late night she'd had the night before.

Her hand hid her smile too, for which she was grateful when she looked up and realised her stepsister Gretchen was watching her, eyes narrowed with curiosity…or mistrust. Probably still smarting after watching Rachel disappear with Damon earlier in the week for the TV studio. And Gretchen had definitely been suspicious when she'd skipped out early on the end of her shift the day before. Rachel had merely said she needed to meet someone—not that she was having afternoon tea at the Ritz, of all places—but even that was unusual enough to raise Gretchen's curiosity.

Her family weren't used to Rachel going places or seeing people. To be honest, Rachel wasn't used to it either. But it looked as if they might all have to grow accustomed to it.

She yawned again and saw Gretchen turn to whisper something to Maisie. Neither of the girls really worked on the shop floor, exactly, but both offered their skills as personal shoppers, and were especially popular at this time of year, when everyone was looking for Christmas party outfits. Rachel knew they were only at the meeting because Hannah insisted on it. She liked to emphasise the family nature of the business as much as possible—and loved it when Rachel showcased the girls in her social media posts for just that reason.

It was also why she took at least one of the staff meetings each week herself, to remind her employees—long term or seasonal—that they were all one big happy family. A family that was expected to work overtime without extra pay, but still family.

At the front of the room, Hannah clapped her hands together and called the meeting to order. The last of the errant staff members edged into the room, letting the door bang closed behind them as she began to speak.

'Good morning, everyone, and thank you for another week's hard work!' She threw a meaningful look at her daughters and the two of them started applauding, the rest of the staff following suit after a few moments. 'Now, the rota for next week's shifts is already up on the system, and I have a printout on the wall over there.' She waved a hand at a spot of wall just behind Rachel.

Gosh, she must have been tired not to notice it there. Usually Rachel relied on the electronic schedule to tell her when she needed to be on the shop floor since she was usually in the building most days anyway, doing the other parts of her job. But after the late night with Damon she'd forgotten to check it since the new rota went up. Now she craned her neck backwards to find her name—and almost let her chair tip over backwards.

What had happened? Normally she only put in occasional shifts on the shop floor, but this week she'd been put down to work there every day. How on earth was she supposed to work at the Cressingham Arcade, do all her social media work for Hartbury's *and* put in so much time behind a till? It simply wasn't going to work.

She had to make a choice.

Did she continue life as normal, here at Hartbury's, and give up on the arcade? Or did she speak out and ask for something different?

When was the last time she had asked her

family for something, rather than the other way round? She couldn't remember. And wasn't that kind of sad, now she thought about it?

She'd always tried to keep the peace. Even when it became clear that the Big Family Experiment her father had signed them up for wasn't the happy families scenario he'd hoped for. He tried so hard to keep all of them on the same page, all getting along, that she'd always felt she had to do the same too. For him.

For her mum, who'd made them promise to look after each other, as she lay dying. Leaving them.

For the dad she remembered from before, when she was little and life was magical.

For herself, even, because it was easier to keep her head down and fade into the background than stretch her head above the parapet and get it chopped off. Metaphorically speaking.

Keeping the peace had become the default—even more so since Dad's health problems had started. The mild heart attack he'd experienced had been the culmination of years of him 'just not feeling right'. The same way her mum had felt 'off' for months before the diagnosis that had changed their lives and stolen her away.

Rachel had been so focussed on making sure her dad was okay that she'd forgotten to even think about what she needed. She'd put off all her own plans—moving out, changing careers—out of fear that he might go downhill as rapidly as her mum had.

But he hadn't. She'd started to think about moving on-until last summer's heart attack had sent her spiralling back again. So now, years after she started worrying about his health, she was still in the same holding pattern, waiting for the next set of test results before she made a move.

Sitting there in another staff meeting, just like all the others, Rachel admitted the truth to herself: there'd be another round of tests after this one. Another reason to be worried about leaving her dad. Another excuse to put off spreading her wings and chasing her own dreams—if she could even decide what they were.

There would *always* be an excuse.

But there might not be another opportunity like the one Damon was offering her. If she wanted it, she had to change things to take it. She had to risk disturbing the hard-earned family peace for once.

She wasn't even asking for much. Just to have a life, and a career, away from the family business. That wasn't unreasonable, was it? Given all the unpaid extra time she put in at Hartbury's anyway, surely she'd earned some time off this festive season.

She just had to gather her courage and ask for it. *The worst they can say is no, right?*

'As ever, if you have any questions or issues with the rota—' Hannah started, and Rachel suddenly made her decision, thrusting her hand up into the air before she could change her mind. 'Rachel?'

'I, uh…' And now she was remembering all the other worse things than them saying no. The pitying looks her stepsisters were giving her, the assumption that she was about to make a fool of herself somehow in front of everybody. How, she had no idea, and probably they didn't either. But it was the same look they'd given her every time she'd ventured an opinion or tried to change something about her little life, ever since she was a teenager.

The same look she'd seen in everyone's eyes last summer when Gretchen's friend Tobias had laughed and told their group that he'd only ever shown interest in her as a joke, or out of pity. Even though she'd known the truth—and also known that he'd never admit it.

'Yes?' Hannah said, impatiently. 'Is this important, or can we discuss it later?'

'I'm down for a shift every day next week, but I'm afraid I have other commitments.' The words came out all in a rush, and Rachel could feel the heat in her cheeks. Which was ridiculous. She was merely asking for a change to the rota, not an invitation to a royal ball.

It was interesting how similar Hannah, Gretchen and Maisie all looked when they each raised their eyebrows in that same look of disbelief.

'"Other commitments"?' Hannah repeated. 'Darling, I'm sure whatever else you have planned can't be more important than our team effort here to make this the best Christmas season Hartbury's has ever seen.' There was a desultory sort of cheer from the staff at that, mostly led by Maisie, as far as Rachel could tell. 'Now, moving on—'

'I was just wondering if there was anyone who would like to switch shifts with me,' Rachel interrupted, her voice wavering a little. 'Someone who might need them more than me.' That made it sound more like a team effort, right?

'Actually…' Across the room, another hand went up. 'I did ask if I could pick up some extra shifts between now and Christmas, but I've only got two shifts next week.'

Rachel spun around to beam at the woman, a seasonal worker, she thought, who had spoken. 'Perfect, then! We can swap!'

At the front of the room, Hannah was glowering at them both. But she couldn't very well object without making a scene, Rachel knew.

'If we've all quite finished messing around with my rota?' she said, her voice sharp. 'Let's get on.'

Smiling to herself, Rachel settled back down in her chair. She'd asked for what she wanted, and she'd got it.

She just hoped her family didn't show too much interest in exactly what her other commitments were.

Damon looked up the few steps to the familiar door of the London town house and sighed.

'Once a month,' he muttered to himself. 'It's only once a month. How bad can it be?'

The black door opened and his sister stuck her head out. 'Are you coming in? Or are you abandoning me to suffer the disappointment and disapproval of our parents alone this month?'

She sounded cheerful enough despite her words so Damon could only assume that the drinks trolley was out at least.

'I'm coming.' Reluctantly, he climbed the steps and shut the door behind him. Shrugging off his coat, he hung it in the small cupboard at the bottom of the stairs, the action firing his memories of doing the same thing a thousand times before—stretching up to try and reach the hooks as a small child, Celeste laughing at him as she reached them easily.

The house was full of memories. A whole childhood's full.

And how he hated reliving any of them.

'Damon. You're late.' His mother pressed a distracted kiss to his cheek as he entered the kitchen.

Handing over the two bottles of wine he'd brought, one white and one red, Damon apologised. 'Sorry. What delights await us at the table today?'

Diana Hunter rolled her eyes. 'Your father is in charge of the main course this month, so he's banished me from the kitchen for most of the day. I've only just been allowed in to check on my dessert. I had to make it yesterday, and of course your sister has brought her starter from home. She's made some sort of salmon terrine, I believe. And I've been experimenting with a walnut and stilton cheesecake—a sort of amalgam of pudding and cheese course in one.'

It sounded foul, although Damon didn't share the thought. And Celeste *knew* he hated salmon. Which made him wonder why she'd picked it; normally it was the two of them against the older generation at these events. If she'd taken against him he was doomed.

He had a horrible suspicion that she must have been talking to Rachel.

'None of them will hold a candle to my pièce de résistance!' Jacob Hunter, broad-chested and booming, emerged from the dining room looking triumphant. 'I am most certain to take the crown, not just this month, but for the whole year, with my main course.'

Because naturally, the monthly family Sunday lunch was a competition, just like everything else in their lives. A chance to prove that they were brighter, better, than each other. At the university, his parents competed academically, Celeste striving to keep up, to surpass them, to show them that she was as clever, as accomplished, as they were. His sister had never realised, in her twenty-eight years, that their parents were simply too busy focussing on their own achievements to ever really appreciate those of their children.

Damon, on the other hand, had realised young that he'd never be the academic genius they expected, or even the sort of person who could focus his talent into a lifelong goal or project. So he'd stopped trying to compete altogether.

He followed his own path instead, one that twisted and splintered as he followed every passing interest, using his entrepreneurial brain to take on varied projects that kept his interest and his bank balance high.

And every month he brought the wine to family dinner, rather than succumbing to the ongoing contest to produce the most interesting dish of the month. Never even the tastiest, just the most interesting.

Salmon terrine was as boring as it got. He was definitely in trouble with Celeste.

His sister reappeared from the dining room also, giving him a knowing look as he passed her.

The table, decorated by Celeste as the person in charge of starters this month, was festooned with candles and golden platters, while what sounded like harp music played through the speaker in the corner.

Damon frowned, trying to put his finger on the theme.

'I was going for Tudor,' Celeste said, eyeing her handiwork. 'But I got distracted at the last minute by a call from Rachel and didn't have time to pick up all the trimmings I wanted.'

A call from Rachel. Well, that wasn't going to be good.

Fortunately, Celeste didn't have time to press the point because at that moment their parents arrived, both in period costume—different periods, but still—and their dad rang the gong to begin dinner.

Damon pushed his salmon terrine around his plate, shredding it into smaller and smaller pieces to hide under the toast crumbs and token salad Celeste had provided, while the rest of the family talked about research papers they'd read, who was in line for the head of faculty position at the university, which professors had already lined up students for their summer archaeological digs, who had got the coveted funding for their latest research… Damon tuned it all out. It was another world to him, one he'd never wanted to belong to.

In the Hunter family, like any family, love was supposed to be unconditional. If asked if they loved their children equally, Damon was pretty sure his parents would look surprised at the very question, and say that of course they did. And maybe, in the abstract, that was true. But in practice...

Love wasn't an abstract emotion, that was what his childhood had taught him. It wasn't something a person said they felt and that was enough to make it true. Love was what a person did, every day. It was attention given, it was focus. Love was when a person cared more about another person than whatever had previously been important in their own life.

He'd seen it with friends, acquaintances. The moment they had a child, or met the love of their life, their previous existence just fell away. Especially when it came to kids. What they'd wanted before suddenly wasn't as important as what their child needed.

Somehow, Diana and Jacob Hunter must have missed that memo.

They'd ticked 'getting married' and 'having children' off their to-do lists early, then gone back to focussing on what they really cared about: their research and their academic careers. And when Celeste had followed in their footsteps they'd been thrilled, totting the child genius around archaeological sites, or to lectures at the British Museum.

They'd guided her career and, as long as her path matched the one they thought she should be taking, all had been well.

Damon, meanwhile, had always known he couldn't match up. So he hadn't even tried.

Starters over, they all marked their meal score-card with their score—Damon gave it a two, because at least the toast had been nice—then sat back to wait for Jacob to return with the main course.

'I saw some of that festive TV show you were associated with, Celeste,' Diana said, her frown disapproving over the fluttering of what he assumed was an authentic replica of a regency fan, to match her dress.

'Uh…really? Where did you see that?' Because of course their parents didn't have anything as pedestrian as a television in their house. Celeste reached across the table for the wine bottle and refilled her mother's glass, as well as her own. Clearly stalling for time. Damon stretched out his legs under the table, crossed his arms over his chest, and waited to see how his sister would talk her way out of this one.

'A colleague sent me a web link to a clip from it.' Diana's fan fluttered a little faster, even as Damon's smile grew. Finding out that Celeste was taking part in a low-brow, populist TV quiz was one thing. Finding out from a colleague was far worse, because that meant that Other People Knew. People who mattered to his parents.

No matter that the colleague probably thought it was a bit of festive fun. The Professors Hunter didn't *do* fun—at least, not when it came to things that mattered, like history or archaeology, their respective specialist subjects.

'Um, which part?' Celeste asked, desperately.

'You, arguing with some gameshow host about how Christmas trees came to be a British tradition.'

Damon couldn't hold in his laughter any more. The argument had been awkward to watch in filming, but through some genius editing the show that had aired two nights before had made it far more entertaining. The whole half-hour quiz show had basically dissolved into Theo and Celeste bickering about festive traditions, and it seemed that social media had lapped it up—in the usual, hypercritical way.

'That link is everywhere, Mum,' he said, earning himself a glare from his sister. 'Have you seen what they're saying about it on Twitter?' He leaned across the table towards Celeste. 'Did you *really* have a make-up lunch with Theo yesterday? The whole of social media is aflame, wondering what's going on between you two.' His favourite conspiracy theory was that Celeste and Theo had been secretly dating for months, and the show just happened to catch a lover's tiff on film. While Damon knew for a fact that wasn't the case, it amused him nonetheless to imagine poor Theo actually *dating* his sister.

Celeste's cheeks flared red, which was an unexpected bonus. He didn't believe there was anything between his sister and the TV star. But the fact that the very idea embarrassed her, well, that suggested a lot of entertaining sibling teasing in his future.

But Celeste rallied quickly. 'Never mind my lunch. Did you *really* take Rachel for afternoon tea at the Ritz?'

'It was for work!' He needed to nip this one in the bud if he wanted to get out of Sunday lunch without a lecture from his big sister. 'She's helping out on my latest project.'

Diana turned her frown on him instead, leaving Celeste smiling smugly. 'Isn't Rachel an English graduate? How is she going to help with your... what was it? Cinema project?'

Of course the only achievement of Rachel's that registered with his mother was her academic one, even though she'd graduated seven years ago. 'The cinema project was two years ago,' was all he said. 'This is a new one.' There was no point explaining to them about the Cressingham Arcade. It just wouldn't register as important, being outside the academic world that mattered so much to them.

Celeste, however, was biting her lower lip—a sure sign that she was thinking. Damon hated it when his sister started thinking; it usually got him into trouble.

'Just…be careful with Rachel, please? I'd hate for you to, well, give her any ideas.'

Like by, say, kissing her? He didn't need Celeste to get him in trouble. He was doing fine by himself.

'It's work,' he repeated, more for his own benefit than hers. 'That's all.'

'Good. Because, to be honest, I think she's always had a bit of a crush on you. I'd hate for you to lead her on, even accidentally.'

A crush? On him? Damon had no idea where Celeste had got that impression from. Even after that night they'd spent hanging out together at university, Rachel had never treated him as anything but her best friend's little brother, rolling her eyes at his escapades the same way Celeste did.

But Celeste knew Rachel better than anyone. And if she was right…

Memories of that kiss crashed through him again, this time with a little more hope than he'd allowed himself until now.

'Just don't break her heart, okay? I know what you're like.' Celeste's words brought that hope plummeting down to the ground again. She was right; that *was* what he was like. Not intentionally, of course. But he wasn't the committed sort—just look at his career, jumping from one thing to the next. His love life was even worse. He didn't *want* to commit himself to anything, to give up the freedom to follow his whims and desires.

Whereas Rachel...she wasn't like him. She'd worked for the family business her whole life, until he came along and dragged her to Cressingham Arcade. She built perfect worlds inside her windows, with perfect mice families living perfect, normal lives.

And that was something he couldn't for a moment let her believe he was capable of giving. Wasn't that why he'd kept away from her before now?

The double doors to the dining room swung open and his father appeared, the white of his Roman-style toga back-lit by the hallway bulbs against the dim candlelight on the table. In his arms was a large platter with what looked like an entire pig on it, apple in mouth and all, surrounded by jellies with apple slices and spices inside.

'Dinner is served!' Jacob announced, holding the platter high, a smug smile on his face.

Damon sank back in his chair and tried not to think about Rachel.

# CHAPTER SEVEN

'WHERE ARE WE GOING?' Rachel asked as she hurried to keep up with Damon's long-legged stride along the busy London street.

'Research trip,' he answered, shortly. Which told her next to nothing at all.

They were miles away from the Cressingham Arcade—in fact, all the way down in South Kensington. As lovely as their arcade was, she couldn't really imagine that the shops there would suddenly start echoing the style—or the prices—of South Ken. So why were they there?

Unless…

One last turn and Damon came to a halt at the V&A in front of a large sign advertising its Victorian Christmas events. Suddenly things started to make sense.

'You want us to put on a Victorian-style Christmas at the Cressingham Arcade?' Rachel could just imagine all the historical inaccuracies Celeste would probably pick up on if they tried.

Damon shrugged. 'It was just an idea. I thought it might give you some inspiration for the window displays.'

He was right. Already, ideas were starting to swirl around in her brain. And who but Celeste really cared if window displays weren't one hundred per cent historically accurate? People knew what a classic Victorian Christmas looked like in their imagination, and that was what she needed to tap into. As long as it *looked* suitably vintage, that was enough. It was the perfect theme to tie all the windows of the arcade together, *and* link up to the building's Victorian origins.

She grabbed Damon's arm and dragged him towards the entrance. 'Come on. I want to see!'

The Victoria and Albert Museum had graced South Kensington's Cromwell Road since 1857, back when it was just the South Kensington Museum. Its name had been changed in 1899, when Queen Victoria herself had officially laid the foundation stone for the new building, in what turned out to be her last official public appearance. Not only was the museum named after the Queen and her Prince Consort, but it dated firmly from their era too. So it was, Rachel decided after reading all this in the information leaflet outside the museum, only right that it should host its own pop-up Victorian Christmas events over the festive season.

They stepped through the gracefully arched doorway into the entrance hall where they were immediately greeted by two women in Victorian period dress. Bonnets, bustles, gloves and all. One carried a basket filled with what looked like Christmas cards. Rachel took one, and opened it to find it full of festive facts of the sort she was sure her best friend would either enjoy or argue with.

'Huh. Did you know that the first Christmas card was sent by the founding director of the V&A, Henry Cole, in 1843?' she asked, reading from the card.

Damon smirked. 'I did not. And I imagine Theo didn't either, until Celeste argued with him about it on screen last week.'

Rachel groaned at the memory of the filming. 'Did you know she had lunch with him on Saturday?'

'Did she tell you that or did you see it on social media?' Damon asked.

'Both.' She'd had a long, weird phone call with her best friend that evening, trying to unravel the confusion of Celeste's sudden acquaintance with Theo—and Rachel's with Damon. She wasn't sure either of them was making much more sense just yet.

But then they turned to enter the John Madejski garden, a rectangular outdoor space in the centre of the museum, with a small lake in the middle, and Rachel forgot all about Celeste, mesmerised by the sight in front of her instead.

The whole quadrangle had been sent back in time, transformed into a Victorian London Christmas market. There were wooden stalls, chestnuts roasting, mulled wine sellers—all in period costume, of course—and vintage entertainment for the kids at the far end. The stalls were selling everything from wooden toys to Christmas crackers.

'The department store of its day?' Damon murmured, as she stared around her, wide eyed.

'I think they might have had department stores already back then,' she whispered back. 'But I like this more.'

'Me too.' He flashed her a quick grin. 'Come on. Let's go and explore.'

Maybe it was the period surroundings, but it felt perfectly natural to take Damon's arm when he offered it. As if she were some kind of Victorian gentlewoman, with hat and fur stole, taking a turn around the quad with her beau—rather than the truth: that she was a scruffy, single twenty-something, with a bobble hat pulled down over her curls and wearing mittens that unbuttoned into fingerless gloves. Her jeans, boots and festive sweater were hardly anything a Victorian lady would be caught dead in, and she'd been meaning to replace her duffle coat for the past two winters, but every time she tried on new coats her stepsisters decided to help so she always abandoned the idea.

But if she didn't really fit into this world, she couldn't help but see Damon as part of it. Sure, he wasn't wearing a hat or carrying a cane or whatever it was Victorian gentlemen would have done. And his hair was probably a little longer than would have been acceptable, just starting to curl over the tops of his ears, and waving over his forehead. But his smart black woollen coat and grey scarf, the suit underneath it, the shoes that somehow still looked polished despite the muck and mush of London's streets after half an inch of snow the night before, they all screamed gentleman.

Rachel had no idea what he was doing here with her.

Well, except for his job, of course. This wasn't about her, it was about the Cressingham Arcade, and how they were going to put it on the map. She had to focus on that.

Celeste had said as much when they'd spoken over the weekend. Rachel had been burbling on about the Cressingham Arcade and what Damon was trying to do there and how she was going to be involved and, even though she'd tried to keep her conversation work focused, there must have been something in her voice. Maybe she had said Damon's name too many times, or in a too specific way. A not work way. Because Celeste had heard everything she wasn't saying, no matter how hard she had worked at not saying it.

'Rach…you know what my brother's like, right? I mean, I think it's great you've found *something* to be excited about, something more interesting than your stepmother's shop. Just be careful, yeah? Make sure it's the work you're excited about, not Damon.'

Because Damon would never be interested in anyone like her. She knew that, better than anyone. She'd laughed off her friend's concerns, reassured her that she knew *exactly* what Damon was like, and she wasn't stupid enough to even fantasise about getting involved with someone like that, thanks.

She wasn't sure Celeste had believed her. She wasn't sure she believed herself.

Not after that kiss. Or the mice and the butterflies and that moment on the balcony…

She shook her head, and tried to refocus on the Victorian market as they paused in front of a small group of carol singers, looking like the image from the front of a Christmas card.

Both of those occasions had happened in the dark, at night. Maybe that was what made the difference. Anything seemed possible in the darkness, didn't it?

It was daytime now, and she was seeing clearly again.

*Time to focus, Rachel.*

She turned back to the carollers and thought about window displays—and definitely not about Damon's lips on hers.

Rachel was totally engrossed by the carol singers. Damon smiled as he watched her focussed stare, her slight frown enough to put one of the choristers in the front row off her line, not that Rachel had noticed. He almost hated to disturb her focus.

He wondered what she was thinking as she listened. Or what she was visualising. A new window display, perhaps? One with carol singers? That could work. Or maybe he should see if he could hire these guys to sing at the reopening. That would definitely go down well with Lady Cressingham, at least. She was a big music fan, he'd learned, although he suspected their tastes differed somewhat. He'd dated an opera singer once, but that was about as close as he'd got to a love of classical music.

Damon touched Rachel's elbow lightly and, when she looked up at him, gestured towards the stall next to them, which was selling hot chocolates and other treats. Her eyes lit up and she nodded so he left her to enjoy the music and joined the queue for drinks instead.

He wasn't entirely sure what had prompted him to invite Rachel to join him on this expedition today. In truth, she wasn't joining him at all. There was pretty much no chance he'd have come here in the first place if it weren't for her. And it wasn't as if he didn't have a mountain of other work to do that wasn't going to magically happen through the power of hot chocolate.

And yet. Here he was.

He'd spotted an article about the event online while catching up on the business news that morning, and just like that he'd abandoned his whole schedule for the day. Luckily, the schedule had been pretty light in the first place, and didn't involve moving any actual meetings—just a phone call that his virtual assistant had pushed back a few hours. But still.

Damon knew he had a reputation for being spontaneous, for acting on whims and not getting tied down to one project, one person, one future. And that reputation was well earned, he wouldn't even try to deny it. But he also knew he wouldn't have been so successful in his career if he couldn't stick with a project through to the end, if he didn't honour his business commitments, show up on time, and prove himself reliable within the context of his work. His family might not see it, his fleeting girlfriends might not appreciate it, but his business was one thing he *was* committed to.

And he'd blown it off to take Rachel Charles to a Victorian Christmas market.

Shuffling forward one more place in the queue, he tried to cut himself a break. *Technically*, this was work. He was working with a colleague to find the best way to promote Cressingham Arcade, exactly as he was contracted to do. Nobody, not even Lady Cressingham, could find a way to object to that, surely?

Except, when he'd seen Lady Cressingham at the arcade that morning, just arriving as he left the small office, she'd raised her eyebrows and given him a knowing look when he'd confessed where he'd be spending the afternoon. And of course he didn't *need* to be here. He could have just told Rachel the event was happening and let her attend on her own.

Damon glanced back over at where Rachel was watching the carol singers, her dark curls escaping from underneath her cream bobble hat, her arms wrapped around herself, wearing that adorable green duffle coat. She probably didn't care if he was here or not. But that wasn't the point.

The point was, he'd *wanted* to bring her.

He'd wanted to see her eyes light up as she spotted the market, wanted to hear her waffle on about the first ever Christmas card, and where the tradition of Christmas trees really came from. The exact same information he'd automatically tune out if Celeste were imparting it, he happily absorbed and discussed with Rachel. Why?

'Sir? Hot chocolate?' Damon blinked, and realised he'd reached the front of the queue. The girl behind the counter had an edge in her voice that suggested it wasn't the first time she'd asked.

'Yes, please. Two. With marshmallows. And cream. And, well, everything, please.' He handed over a twenty-pound note with his patented charming smile and watched as the server's hostility melted away.

If only it were as easy with Rachel.

Oh, it wasn't that she was actively hostile to him—she never had been, not even when he *knew* she was disapproving of his antics when he had visited them in university. Rachel wasn't really the hostile sort. She just…faded into the background, and let the world happen around her instead. Had he ever realised that before? He wasn't sure. It seemed to him that throughout their whole acquaintance, Rachel had just sort of been there, never drawing attention to herself, never making a fuss, never speaking up, not when Celeste or her family or even Damon himself was there to do it for her.

He'd never really paid her much attention,

except as his sister's best friend. Apart from that one night when they talked until the sun came up.

And that was why, he admitted to himself. That was why he'd pushed her to the sidelines of his mind the same way she kept to the sidelines at parties. Because it was too easy to open up to Rachel, too easy to let her in. Too easy to fall for her.

So he'd kept away. Until now.

What had changed? The obvious answer was that he'd kissed her, Damon supposed. Except he'd kissed a hell of a lot of women, and never once had it compelled him to take them to a Victorian Christmas market before. Or show them all his favourite secret places at Cressingham Arcade under the cover of darkness.

And anyway, he knew it hadn't started with that kiss. It had started hours before that. With a dress, a window and a mouse.

He could pinpoint precisely the moment he stopped forcing himself to see Rachel as nothing more than a quiet extension of his sister. It wasn't when he had realised her stepsisters were trying to humiliate her, so he'd bought her the dress. It wasn't even when he had seen her in that dress and thought how bloody gorgeous she was. It was in between.

It was the moment he'd bent down to look in that shop window and seen a whole hidden world, one that Rachel had created and only shared with those willing to look a little deeper, a little longer.

And he'd been looking deeper and longer at her ever since. He couldn't stop himself any more. Those damn mice had broken down a wall he'd spent the best part of a decade building higher.

He'd spent days thinking about Rachel and that dress, that kiss, that moment on the balcony looking at the butterflies…and he wasn't an inch closer to knowing what to do about it. Especially since he didn't know what *she* wanted him to do about it.

If it was anybody else, he'd ask her outright. But Rachel wasn't just anybody. And for all he knew, actually asking her if she wanted him to kiss her again would only make the situation worse, especially if he embarrassed her or flustered her. She wasn't like the usual women he dated, and he was at a loss to know how to handle her.

Except for the fact that he knew he had to be careful. Not just of her heart, but of his too.

He wasn't about to change his whole life and philosophy just because Rachel Charles made cute window displays. Or even because she kissed like his dreams and because he loved listening to her talk.

It was too easy to let Rachel into his mind, and his heart. It might be hard to get her out again when he wanted to go back to his real life, once this project was over.

Telling the server to keep the change—and earning himself a genuine smile in the process—Damon took the two cups of hot chocolate, laden with chocolate shavings, marshmallows and a lot of whipped cream, and headed back to where he'd left Rachel. She'd barely moved, he realised, still mesmerised by the music. Or so he assumed, until he got close enough to realise that she was muttering to herself under her breath.

He knew he shouldn't listen. That he should tell her he was there. But then, Damon had never been very good at doing what he *should* do.

He edged closer, just enough to make out the words as the carollers finished one song and prepared to break into another.

'Do not read anything into the fact he's buying you a hot chocolate. This is work. It's just cold and he's nice. That's all. Do *not* read anything into it.'

*Huh.*

Maybe he wasn't the only one who'd been obsessing over the last week…

And maybe, just maybe, if he was careful, he might be able to find a way to do something about that. Before he drove himself crazy.

'Hot chocolate?' He smiled as Rachel spun around, horror in her wide eyes, careful to give her no sign at all that he'd overheard her personal pep talk. Instead, he held out the cup and she took it, the horror giving way to wariness, then a smile that made his pulse tick just a little faster as she spotted the whipped cream and toppings.

'Thanks.' Her voice was warm in the freezing air, a little husky even. Sexy. Damon couldn't help but imagine some of the other ways he could make her sound like that, given half the chance.

But not yet, he reminded himself, as Rachel turned back to listen to the carollers begin their next song.

He needed to think this through. For once, he couldn't just rush in. Not until he was completely sure he had a way back out of it again.

It hadn't even been a full week since Rachel started work at Cressingham Arcade, but already the place was starting to feel like home.

Changing her shifts at Hartbury's had given her plenty of free afternoons—and evenings— to spend at the arcade, figuring out what made the place tick, why it was special, and getting new ideas for how she could communicate that to Londoners at large. She'd spent time with each of the shopkeepers individually, looking through their stock, discussing display ideas, taking photos with her heavy Canon camera, and then spending hours looking through them on her laptop screen in Damon's office after the arcade was closed.

Yes, Damon's office. Her cheeks felt warm just thinking about how many evenings she'd spent sitting opposite him in that tiny room, each working on their own laptops on opposite sides of the small desk, as if they were partners, or a pair—

Rachel pulled herself up sharply. Four nights. Less, really, since tonight was only halfway done, and she wasn't even in his office. Three and a half, then, since they'd returned to the arcade after the Victorian market and got to work. That was definitely not enough nights to start getting moony about.

Although…

As much as she was trying to be reasonable and rational about it all, and remember Celeste's warnings—not to mention her own common sense—she had to admit, Damon had seemed… different, this week. Before the fake New Year's Eve party their interactions had been limited at best. They were friendly, of course, but she wouldn't have really called them friends.

Now… Now he knew how she liked her hot chocolate—with as many toppings as possible—and would bring her one from the coffee shop just outside the arcade whenever she was working late. He'd pore over images with her, deciding which ones best represented the shops, even when she was trying to decide between two almost identical photos. He'd listen to her ideas and smile and nod and he didn't talk over her or try to change the subject.

And yes, she knew that all of those things were work related—well, apart from the hot chocolate, perhaps, although for all she knew he was only providing that because he felt guilty about her working late. She knew she should keep reminding herself that this was a working relationship. That Damon had never shown any sign of returning her crush in the ten years she'd known him, apart from that one misguided kiss at fake midnight.

But still…it *felt* different. And Rachel wasn't at all sure what that meant, or what to do about it.

Which was why she was hiding out in the large bay window of the first shop in the arcade—the new stationery and invitation shop, owned by Penelope—fiddling with the first of her displays. Penelope had long since disappeared with her boyfriend, Zach, a huge Viking of a guy with the most besotted smile Rachel had ever seen on a man, leaving Rachel in peace and quiet to create. Or, as she was doing now, procrastinate.

She'd finished the window almost an hour ago, according to her initial design. It looked exactly as she'd pictured in her head too. From the Victorian writing desk in the corner, with inkwell and parchment, to the vintage-style papers she'd used to create the decorations that hung from the ceiling into the window. A Christmas tree made out of paper covered in swirly calligraphy—thanks to Penelope's notebooks and the photocopier in the office—sat in the centre, surrounded by boxes wrapped in the Victorian Christmas card design wrapping paper she was selling inside. A stack of style notebooks from the stock with one open on top, a perfectly matched pen sitting on the page titled 'Christmas Wish List'. There were fairy lights strung around giving it a magical air and the wooden floor sparkled with added stars and glitter too. It looked beautiful.

And yet…

Rachel sighed. It wasn't right. It was everything she'd planned, but maybe she'd got the plan wrong. She'd felt so inspired after the Victorian market and she'd been full of plans to make each window specific to the business, but still with a period twist—just as she'd done for Penelope's shop.

So what was wrong with it?

She stepped back into the shop and squinted at it, trying to identify the problem. But of course, she was looking at it from the wrong angle. She needed to go out into the arcade and look in, really. Except, if she went out she might bump into Damon and that was something else that wasn't quite right. So she stayed where she was and glared at the display until a rap on the window made her jump.

Clutching a hand to her chest, Rachel looked up to see Damon grinning at her through the glass. He beckoned her outside and she went. Apparently avoiding having to deal with this… weirdness between them wasn't an option any more.

Standing shoulder to shoulder, they both looked in at the window display.

'It looks great,' Damon said, and Rachel pulled a face. 'No, it really does. It's perfect for Penelope.'

She could hear the 'but', even if he wasn't saying it. He'd given her this chance and she'd let him down already. Her first attempt at something outside the family business and she couldn't do it.

Steeling herself, she said it for him. 'But?'

He glanced down at her, his expression serious. 'Where are the mice?'

Realisation flowed through her like mulled wine. Of course! *That* was what was missing!

'I was trying to do a grown-up window, something new. And I focussed so hard on the shop and Penelope and the arcade and the Victorian details…'

'You forgot to put some of *you* in it,' Damon

finished, with a gentle smile. 'But that's why I hired you, remember? Because I wanted *your* style. I want *you*.'

Oh, and didn't those words hit her right where it tingled?

But he didn't mean it like that. He meant the window display. Narrowing her eyes, Rachel studied it again, this time letting her imagination overlay reality, until she could picture exactly how it should look. Tiny felted mice, maybe in brightly coloured jackets, scurrying over the parcels, tightening ribbons and tying bows, or lifting a pen to write their own wish list in a mini notebook on top of the real one. The whole scene brought to life the way she hadn't been able to make it tonight. It would take her a while to make enough mice, but felting the creatures was relaxing and she could do it in front of the telly in her bedroom, so it would be fine. And it would be worth it.

Because the display really would feel like hers.

She wouldn't hide the mice away this time; she didn't need to. But maybe she'd leave a hint for the children to look for the secret mice Damon had shown her, just for fun.

Bouncing on her toes a little, she turned to Damon, beaming. 'I know *exactly* how it needs to look now. And I can carry it through to the other windows too...' A Victorian-style mouse

Christmas. It would be perfect. She couldn't wait to get started.

Damon had other ideas, though.

'Great! In that case, I'm taking you for dinner.' Her breath caught at his words. What was this? A date? Or just a working dinner? Then he went on, 'You've been at this for hours; you need more than just hot chocolate tonight,' and she understood.

He was looking after her, probably at Celeste's request. That was all.

She looked back at her window, and thought about her mice. Then she thought about dinner with Damon. Old Rachel would be hiding away making mice already by now, staying far away from temptation or opportunity or potential embarrassment.

But ever since that kiss, she hadn't felt so much like Old Rachel any more. She felt like someone new. Someone who, perhaps, might take a chance once in a while.

Gesturing down at her leggings and jumper, she smiled ruefully at Damon. 'As long as you're not planning on eating anywhere with a dress code.'

His smile was warm, friendly. 'Don't worry. I know the perfect place.'

# CHAPTER EIGHT

DAMON WATCHED RACHEL'S face light up as they approached the café with its outdoor tables and heaters, and the chairs with the rugs and blankets layered over the back for warmth. He'd been right. This was perfect for…whatever the hell this was between them.

As much as he'd love to treat her to a fancy restaurant—one of the stupidly expensive ones where paparazzi took photos of every patron because, really, they had to be *someone* to be dining there, even if the person behind the camera didn't recognise them—that wasn't them. It wasn't Rachel and, honestly, it wasn't really him either.

Luciana's, however, was.

'Ah! Mama's best customer, here again.' Tony, Luciana's twenty-something son, rolled his eyes at Damon as he led them to his usual table. 'Do I need to worry about my mother's virtue?'

'Only her lasagne,' Damon assured him.

Tony clicked his tongue as he pulled out a chair for Rachel. 'I won't tell her you're only interested in her for her food. It would break her heart.' Handing them both menus, he disappeared to deal with another couple of customers looking at the board by the entrance.

Damon turned his attention back to his dinner companion, and found her staring at him.

He paused in taking his own seat. 'Is this…is this okay?' Maybe the thing about no dress code had been a joke. Maybe she really had been expecting one of those fancy restaurants. But no, she'd looked excited when they arrived. What had changed?

'It's perfect.' Rachel shook her head, just a little. 'I love Italian, and this place is darling. Plus no one is going to notice the dust from the window all over my leggings once I'm snuggled under this blanket.'

Damon sat, still not convinced. 'Then what is it? You look…confused.' Was that the right word? He wasn't sure. He was normally good at reading people—their expressions, their moods, even their thoughts, to a point. But Rachel seemed to surprise him at every turn.

'I just assumed you brought me here because, well, you thought it was more…my level, I guess. The sort of place I'd belong.' She shrugged as if her words meant nothing, but Damon could hear the echoes of pain in her voice. 'I never imagined it would be somewhere you'd come regularly.'

He didn't push her on her original assumption— he could tell she was uncomfortable about having to say it out loud in the first place. But he did question the second part of her statement, not least because it echoed his own thoughts from earlier.

'You thought I only frequented the uber-fashionable London restaurants, huh? The ones where people go just to be seen?'

Rachel raised her eyebrows, just a little. 'Given how many times you *have* been seen at them, can you blame me?'

That was more like it. Those sparks of amusement, of life, that he'd grown used to seeing in Rachel over the last week or so were back.

'Trust me,' he said, setting aside the menu. He already knew it off by heart anyway. 'I only go to those places because the people I'm dining with want to eat there. When it's just me, I come here and eat Luciana's lasagne. Or sometimes her risotto of the day. It's comfort food for me.'

And so unlike the elaborate dishes his family insisted on cooking—or the ready meals or cereal he'd grown up on, since when they weren't trying to impress each other, or other people, his parents were generally too busy to bother cooking at all.

Luciana cooked food she liked and gave it to people hoping they would like it too. It was that simple and refreshing.

'How did you find it?' Rachel wasn't looking at the menu either, he realised. She was focused entirely on him.

'I stumbled on it a few years ago and promptly offered over my soul in return for a regular table and lasagne whenever I needed it.'

That earned him a thwack on the head with the menu from behind. He didn't need to look up to know who was responsible for it.

'Luciana, my love.' With a quick smile at Rachel, he turned around to charm the restaurant's owner, head chef, and matriarch of the family business back onto his side again. 'You know I think it was a perfectly fair price for lasagne as incredible as yours.'

Luciana rolled her eyes. 'Like I'd want your soul. Who knows where that thing has been?' She shot Rachel a sympathetic look. 'All I accepted from him was the occasional suggestion for improving our business. Mostly stuff I'd have done anyway, but he looked like he needed feeding, poor little boy. Now, are you two ready to order?'

Rachel appeared to stifle a giggle at the 'poor little boy' comment, but he was pretty sure she could read between Luciana's lines as well as he could. The restaurant had been on the verge of closure before he'd walked in that first night. The fact it was now bustling and busy on a Thursday night in December, with even all the outdoor tables occupied, brought him more satisfaction than any of the bigger, more corporate projects he'd done recently.

They both ordered the lasagne—Rachel without even looking at the menu.

'You didn't want to see what else there was on offer?' he asked as Luciana retreated back to the kitchen.

Rachel shrugged. 'You said the lasagne was best. I trust your judgement.'

It was a throwaway comment, Damon knew, one that didn't mean anything more than that she fancied lasagne. But still, hearing Rachel say she trusted his judgement…it meant something more to him, somehow. That someone from outside his business world, someone who was more connected to his sister, his family, than his corporate achievements, trusted his judgement…

Damon smiled, slowly. 'You won't be disappointed,' he promised.

And he really hoped he could keep it, long after the lasagne was finished.

Luciana's was Rachel's new favourite restaurant. By the time she'd swallowed her first mouthful of lasagne she'd already decided she'd be coming back again, soon and often. With or without Damon.

But, oh, she hoped it was with.

She didn't exactly have a lot of experience of dating. She'd been on a few dates, of course, but they'd mostly been awkward affairs she'd been happy to get over and done with. But tonight?

Sitting in a tiny pedestrianised square in London, at a café table with a fluffy blanket around her shoulders, eating lasagne, sipping red wine and laughing about the world…it felt like every romantic fantasy she'd ever had. Which probably said more about the feebleness of her fantasy life than she'd like.

She'd been so sure that this was just another 'friends and colleagues' dinner. But as the evening wore on and the wine took effect, she wondered. She looked into Damon's laughing eyes and remembered for the millionth time how it had felt to kiss him after so many years of imagining it.

And she wanted it again.

'So, what do you want to do now?' Damon asked as she finished off the last spoonful of tiramisu. 'Ready for home or…?'

He trailed off. It didn't matter, though. Rachel could hear worlds of possibility in his words.

She should go home. She had dozens of felt mice to make, not to mention the fact that she was behind on the Hartbury's social media because she'd been giving so much time and attention to the arcade.

More than that, she knew that going home now was the least risky strategy. The one that protected her heart and stopped her getting *Ideas*, with a capital I. The longer she spent with Damon this way, the closer she got to believing there could be something more than friendship between them.

And yet…

'Or?' Rachel picked up her almost empty glass of wine. It had to be the alcohol giving her the confidence to ask what her other options were. Heavens knew she'd never manage it on her own.

Damon's smile turned warmer somehow. More seductive. She could feel herself falling into his eyes…

'Carol singing.' He pushed his chair back from the table, leaving her blinking.

'What?'

'It's still early.' Holding out a hand, Damon pulled her to her feet. 'And they're singing carols in Trafalgar Square this evening. If we leave now we could just about make it. Come on!'

He flung some notes down on the table, waved a goodbye to Luciana and her son, and dragged Rachel back out onto the busy London street that had seemed miles away while they ate.

Carol singing. Really?

'So is this something else you secretly do all the time?' she asked as they hurried along the pavement, while she tried to match his long stride with her much shorter legs.

'Only in December,' he deadpanned. Then he smirked at her. 'No, it's not. But…'

'But?' she pressed, when it became clear he wasn't going to finish the thought.

'But I wasn't ready to say goodnight to you just yet.' Suddenly, the December air no longer seemed cold.

There was such heat in his eyes as he looked down at her, Rachel felt it flooding through her skin into her blood.

That heat. Even Rachel knew what it meant, although it wasn't something she was used to seeing in men's eyes when they looked at her. She could feel the truth of it in her bones, and the relief of knowing she wasn't the only one soothed her jagged edges.

She knew Damon charmed everyone. Knew his easy smiles and his warm looks didn't mean anything. Understood that even their unexpected kiss was just another part of who Damon was. Celeste had warned her but she hadn't needed to, not really. Rachel had watched Damon through their university years, and after, from the periphery as always. She knew who Damon was.

But she'd never had it turned on her before. All that charm. Those smiles.

Right now, she understood all those girls who fell for him one weekend then spent the next week crying on the sofa in their flat after he let them down.

She wasn't one of those girls, though. She knew better. And not just because she knew Damon. She'd been here before. With Tobias, Gretchen's friend, who'd turned on the charm and turned out to be a liar. Or maybe just a coward. With other men who thought she might be a good way to get closer to her stepsisters—and presumably their bed sheets. Apart from Tobias, she'd never been stupid enough to believe any of them. But that didn't mean they hadn't tried. Gretchen and Maisie were beautiful, rich, desirable. Rachel knew she was none of those things, and so did the men who lied to her and tried to convince her otherwise, just to get close to the women they *really* wanted.

As if being close to Rachel would give them an advantage when it came to her stepsisters. It was laughable, but Rachel supposed the guys didn't know how much Gretchen and Maisie despised her.

Oh, they tried to hide it. Tried to pretend they were fond of her, in a 'poor Rachel' way. That they were helping her with their hideous clothing suggestions. Maybe they really thought they were. To start with, Rachel had believed it too.

She knew better now, even if she didn't say so. Always keeping the peace for her father's sake, that was her. He was all she had left; she couldn't risk anything else.

But Damon… She knew Damon. He wouldn't try to hurt her. He wasn't trying to get close to her stepsisters. He genuinely seemed to enjoy her company. The charm and the smiles…they were just a part of him, something he couldn't switch off. He'd used those on her back in university too; that was what had kickstarted her crush after that night they'd spent just the two of them. But the connection between them, the fizz and the pull she'd felt since their kiss, that was something else.

Something she was starting to believe he might feel too.

It defied explanation but that didn't mean it wasn't happening.

Damon Hunter wanted her. Whether he meant to or not.

Now she just had to decide what to do about it—and how to protect her heart in the process.

Because wanting, she knew only too well, wasn't loving. And it would be all too easy for her to fall if she wasn't careful.

But it could also be something else. The next step to finding her freedom…?

She'd already jumped, hadn't she? Taking the job at the Cressingham Arcade, preparing for a life outside the claustrophobic family bubble she'd been caught in for too long. One where she could chase her own dreams, for a change, rather than always keeping the peace and keeping quiet.

Perhaps a fling with Damon was just what she needed to give her the confidence to take the next move towards the future she'd been dreaming of for too long.

* * *

Carol singing. What the hell had he been thinking?

Well, he knew the answer to that. He'd been thinking that he wasn't ready for the evening to end—and that Rachel wasn't exactly the sort of girl he could just invite up to his flat for a nightcap. And now, here they were, crushed into the crowd at Trafalgar Square, singing carols. Or silently mouthing the words in his case. It was nobody's Christmas miracle hearing his appalling singing voice.

Rachel had been thoughtful on the walk over, quieter than he was used to, although even that thought stopped him in his tracks. Rachel had *always* been quiet and thoughtful. That was who she was. But this week, working together, eating together, drinking hot chocolate together…he'd seen a different side to her. A more lively, talkative one that he suspected few people besides Celeste ever really got to see.

It made him feel…privileged. Special.

Lucky.

She wasn't quiet now, either. Holding up her carol sheet, she was singing loudly, her voice ringing in his ears despite all the others around them, beautiful and clear. Her eyes shone with festive joy and Damon silently thanked whatever impulse had led him to bring her here.

Maybe it had been memory. A long-hidden

memory of a Christmas at the university, swinging his legs sitting on his mother's desk while he waited for her to finish up work. He wasn't sure where his father had been—away, perhaps. That had been the case more often than not, back then. But it must have been Christmas, because he'd heard carols ringing down the hallways and he'd wanted to hear more. He'd slipped off the desk and followed the sound, finding the university choir rehearsing for their Christmas concert. He'd stayed and listened, mesmerised, until his mother had found him.

She'd dragged him out of there and her words had stayed with him every bit as much as the music. *'There's no point listening to that. None of our family have ever been able to hold a tune in a bucket. You're not going to be a famous musician, Damon, so don't waste your time.'*

Because in his family, the only things worth time were the things they could excel at. Could be the best at.

Damon hadn't wanted to be the best. He'd just wanted to listen to the music.

He pushed away the thought and focussed on the here and now. The carols filling the square. And Rachel, singing unselfconsciously next to him.

He wanted to see this Rachel more often. The one who sparkled when she smiled at him. The one who pulsed with delight at hidden mice and butterflies. The one who melted in his arms when he kissed her.

He definitely wanted to see more of that one.

But how could he without ruining the friendship and working partnership they'd built up? Without hurting her when she realised he couldn't live up to whatever she was expecting from him?

Rachel didn't do meaningless flings, Celeste had been clear on that. And could anything between them be meaningless anyway? They'd been friends for a decade, even if mostly through Celeste. That had meaning.

He didn't do serious, or commitment, or anything that tied him down beyond his limited attention span. So, as far as he could see, he was right back where he'd been nine years ago, when he'd pulled away from her after a night of closeness, because he knew how easy it would be for him to get drawn into Rachel's orbit—and how hard it might be to escape from it, afterwards. They were at an impasse.

An impasse that had resulted in carols in Trafalgar Square, somehow.

A sharp elbow in his ribs, mildly painful even through two layers of coats, broke his train of thought.

'You're not singing,' Rachel said, speaking out

of the side of her mouth, her eyes still on her carol sheet.

'Trust me, that's for everyone's benefit,' he murmured back. 'Have you ever heard me sing?'

'No, actually.' She turned her head to study him, looking honestly surprised to have found some new aspect to his character that she hadn't considered before. 'Are you really dreadful?'

'Terrible,' he admitted.

'Worse than Celeste?'

'Well, I wouldn't go that far...'

Rachel laughed at that, then turned back to her carol sheet as the introduction for the next song was played by the small band at the centre of the square. She shivered a little as she did so, Damon noticed.

'Are you cold? Shall I fetch you a hot chocolate?'

She glanced back at him again. 'No. I'm still full from the tiramisu.'

'Do you want my coat?'

Her brow creased with confusion. 'No, because then you'll freeze. I'm fine, Damon.'

Except she wasn't. He touched a hand to her face and found it icy. Clearly she was frozen, but she didn't want to leave. And for reasons he wasn't studying too closely right now, it was very important to him that Rachel not be cold. Or uncomfortable. Or unhappy at all.

Well, if she wouldn't take his coat, he'd just have to warm her up another way.

He moved slowly, giving her plenty of time to object if she wanted to. The slightest sound or reaction from her and he'd have given up the idea completely. But as he stepped into her space, standing behind her, and wrapped his arms around her waist, he felt her melt against him. As if she was meant to be there.

'What are you doing?' she whispered, missing the next line of the carol.

'Keeping you warm, so you can keep singing.'

She didn't respond to that. But a moment later he heard her sweet voice raised in song again and he smiled.

By the time the carols were over, Damon knew it was time to call it a night. That he should be seeing Rachel home safely, then going home to bed himself. Alone.

He just didn't want to.

And he was starting to think that Rachel didn't want to, either.

She turned around within the circle of his arms until her breasts were pressed against his chest and she was looking directly up into his eyes. He could loosen his hold, he supposed, but that might mean she moved further away. He really didn't want that to happen.

'So,' she said, her voice soft, the cold air turning to steam around her words. 'What's next?'

'You're not tired?' he asked, desperately hopeful.

She shook her head. 'I don't want to call it a night yet. Do you?'

'No,' he admitted. He had a horrible feeling they were going to have to talk about it at some point. And that talking would probably bring it to an end. But for now... 'How about we grab a drink?'

'Good idea.'

It was easy enough to find a pub with a small corner table free where they could warm up some more and talk without interruption. Damon fetched them both drinks then eased his body between the wall and the table to sit in the narrow booth seat across from Rachel.

She took her glass of wine, her brow furrowed as she stared down at it, her lower lip caught between her teeth. Slowly, she twisted the glass round and round on the wood of the table, obviously lost in thought.

And he... well. He just watched her think. Because he liked looking at her. Because he liked imagining what *she* might be imagining. Wondrous scenes for the arcade windows, perhaps. Or remembering the carols in the square. Or Luciana's lasagne.

Or even, maybe, him.

Was that just wishful thinking? Damon had assumed so, until Celeste's comment at Sunday lunch about Rachel having had a crush on him. And since then he'd been watching very closely. If she had, she had hidden it well—until tonight.

Tonight, she'd sunk into his embrace as if it was where she belonged. And every moment she'd stayed there, that hope had grown. And when she'd said she wasn't ready to call it a night…

He'd been afraid that talking about what he felt growing between them would make her shut it down. Now, suddenly, he was afraid that ignoring it might scare it away. Or let Rachel think her way out of acknowledging it at all.

*She doesn't know how to ask for what she wants.*

The realisation hit hard but he knew instinctively it was the truth. Just as she hadn't been able to tell her stepsisters which dress she actually liked, or how she hadn't put any of her mice in the window at the arcade until he'd suggested it. When she'd recounted the story of asking for fewer shifts at the department store, what had struck him most was how unusual it had been for her to ask in the first place. And how her family hadn't seemed to listen anyway.

Well. That was going to be a problem. Because there was no way Damon was going to do *any-*

*thing* about the attraction between them unless she told him she wanted him to.

Which meant getting her talking.

'What are you thinking about?' It was a classic, but it made Rachel's gaze shoot up to meet his.

'What do you mean?' She sounded flustered, her eyes wide, and suddenly he wondered if anybody *ever* asked her what was on her mind. Seemed to him, mostly they wanted to tell her what they *thought* she should be thinking instead.

He wasn't going to be that guy.

'You look like there's something on your mind, that's all,' he said nonchalantly, hoping it wasn't obvious how desperate he was for that something to be him. 'Want to tell me what it is?'

He could see her steeling herself to speak, as if her courage were a coat she was pulling on. For half a second, he felt bad for making her do this, then he realised that, no, that wasn't how he felt at all.

He felt proud of her for trying. For whatever she said next. For having the guts to ask for what she wanted, when no one in her life ever seemed to have listened before.

Then she said, 'I want you to come to my work Christmas party with me tomorrow night. Will you?' And he started rethinking everything all over again.

# CHAPTER NINE

WHY HAD SHE asked that? Oh, *why* had she asked that?

Rachel considered just hiding under the pub table but, really, the words were out now so what was the point?

It was obvious that whatever Damon had been expecting her to say, it hadn't been that. All the same, he rallied rapidly and tossed her a smile as he picked up his pint.

'That depends,' he said, before taking a sip.

'On what?' He probably had plans. *Of course* he'd have plans. It was a Friday night two weeks before Christmas. *Everybody* had plans. Hell, even *she* had plans, which meant that there couldn't be another person in London who didn't.

'Will you wear the dress I bought you?' He raised one eyebrow as he asked, a smirk hovering around his lips.

Rachel's breath caught, rendering her unable to answer. Which was just as well, since she had no idea what to say. It felt like a tease, like a joke she was too socially awkward to understand,

and from anybody else, especially the guys in her stepsisters' social circle, she'd be certain it was.

But this was *Damon*. And as much as he might look and act like those guys on the surface, she was almost certain that underneath he wasn't. Almost.

She took a chance. 'Do you…want me to?'

He grinned. 'Definitely. You looked gorgeous in that dress last week.'

When he'd kissed her. Oh, no.

'Then…yes, I could wear that dress.'

'Then it's a date.' His grin suddenly faltered. 'Wait. That's not what I meant.'

Of course not. As if Damon Hunter would ever go on an actual date with her. At least he was sweet enough to make sure she hadn't got the wrong idea. *Unlike Tobias.*

'No, of course, I didn't think—' she started, shaking her head as if she could simply shake away any idea of a relationship with Damon.

Then she realised he was still speaking.

'Unless you wanted it to be a date.'

Her head shot up, her gaze hitting his, looking for any hint of deception or humour in his eyes.

She found none.

'What do you mean?' Because none of this was making any sense to her any more.

Reaching across the table, Damon took her hand. 'I'm saying this all wrong.'

'What happened to that patented Hunter charm?'

'Apparently it doesn't work with you,' he said, and Rachel just about resisted the urge to tell him how very, very wrong he was about that.

She sighed. 'Did you mean that I might want it to be a pretend date?' It was her best guess, the only way she could really make sense of his contradictory statements. 'You know, to make it look like I actually have a date in front of my stepsisters?' Because actually that didn't sound so bad.

But Damon looked horrified at the very idea. 'No!'

'Why not?' Rachel asked, before she could stop herself. 'It sounds like just the sort of fun trick I'd have thought you'd love, from Celeste's stories.'

She laughed, as if it could cover how painfully awkward this whole conversation was.

Damon didn't laugh, though. Instead, he reached across the table and took her hands in his. 'Because it wouldn't be pretend. I want—' He broke off, and sighed. 'I promised myself—I promised Celeste, come to that, and she's much scarier than my own guilt—that I wouldn't do anything that could hurt you. After that kiss, I told myself that the only way it could happen again was if you asked for it. But I realised tonight… you'd never ask, would you?'

Eyes wide, Rachel shook her head. She *wouldn't* ask. Because she couldn't imagine for a moment that he would say yes. Even on the walk over, imagining a fling with him, at least half her brain had still been assuming it was a fantasy brought on by too much wine and lasagne.

'But I wanted you to. And it turns out… I'm still no good at obeying the rules, even the ones I set myself.' He took a deep breath and Rachel was amazed to see something that looked like nervousness in his smile. 'So, Rachel Charles, I'd love to go to your work party with you. As a friend, or a colleague if you'd like. Or as your date, if you'll have me.'

Her world spun and it had nothing to do with the wine. Damon Hunter had asked her on a date. Her decade-long fantasy was becoming reality, and her first thought was…

*What's the catch?*

Because as much as she liked Damon, she knew she wasn't his usual type. He looked as blindsided by this weird attraction between them as she was. And that, more than anything, reminded her of a truth she'd already internalised.

*I could get hurt here, if I'm not careful. Heartbroken.*

And that wasn't a risk she was willing to take. This couldn't be like Tobias again, with him in control, the one deciding when they were together or not, the one keeping her a secret from all his friends. She didn't believe Damon would disown her in public the way Tobias had, pretending it was all a great joke. But she also knew Damon had the power to hurt her in other ways. She'd wanted him for so long, how would she feel when he didn't want her any more, after she'd tasted what being with him could be like?

*I can protect my heart. As long as I know what I'm getting into.*

Rachel always had a plan, and she plodded through it one step at a time. It might be boring but it was what she needed here too.

Next to freedom, the thing she wanted most was everything that Damon could offer her. But it had to be on her own terms. Her plan, not his.

Which meant she had to suck it up and ask for what she needed. Damon had done the hardest part for her. Now she just had to make sure she protected her heart well enough that, when the clock struck midnight on this thing between them, she wasn't left broken in a corner somewhere regretting her life choices.

She had to speak up for once.

Releasing her fingers from his grip, she reached for her wine, took a fortifying sip, then made herself say the words.

'If this is going to be a date, there have to be ground rules.'

He looked amused at that. She just hoped he was still smiling by the time she'd finished.

The Hartbury's Christmas Party was supposed to be the highlight of the department store's staff calendar, but as far as Damon could see that didn't say much for the rest of the year's events.

'They don't even bother to hire somewhere for the party?' he muttered to Rachel as they joined the queue to get inside the department store.

Rachel shrugged. 'Hannah always says there's no point, since they already have all this space, and venue-hire costs are astronomical at this time of year. Although Dad did try to persuade her to move it a couple of years ago after one of the seasonal workers was sick inside one of the display mannequins.'

He shot her a confused look. 'Inside?'

She nodded. 'They're hollow, you see. Apparently he just took the torso off, threw up down the legs, then put it back on again. We didn't find it for days after the smell started to spread.'

'That's…horrible.'

'Yep. And if that didn't convince her to move the party somewhere else, I don't reckon anything will.'

The queue was filled with staff members who spent all their working days at the shop and who were now heading back there in their glad rags for the party. Damon wasn't sure he'd have bothered, if he were them.

But he wasn't really thinking about them. He was thinking about the woman standing beside him, holding his hand in her gloved one.

Holding hands. He felt about fourteen again, obsessing about a girl's hand in his. Rachel did that to him. Stripped away all those years of experience and left him uncertain and unsure again in a way he hadn't even been when he *met* her, all those years ago.

He wasn't sure he liked it.

But he liked *her*. Which was why he was happy to be here, at her side, despite his awful sense of foreboding about this party as a whole. And despite—or perhaps because of—her ground rules.

He'd been afraid she'd expect too much from him, things he wasn't able to give, like promises and commitment. Instead, she'd leaned across the table and asked for the opposite.

*'This is a Christmas fling,'* she'd said, her face serious. *'I am not expecting for ever, and I know you're not either. This is fun, that's all. Because there's obviously something between us and I think I'd like to explore that a bit. But we both have to be very clear on one thing: this is over the moment the last Christmas cracker has been pulled.'*

*'Are you sure?'* he'd asked, hardly able to believe she was speaking his own thoughts to him so clearly.

She was giving him the way out he needed, setting the boundaries that would allow him to move on when he needed to. Because he always needed to, he knew that about himself.

Her answering smile had lit him up inside.

*'Very. I've never had a proper fling before— not one that counted. You can be my first.'*

Except, of course, fling clearly meant something different to Rachel than to most people. And he wasn't going to push her a second faster than she wanted to go. So he'd put her in the taxi with a chaste kiss goodnight, and now here he was, one night later, holding her hand like a prom date.

But it would be worth it. Even if he never tempted her up to his bedroom before she called time on their fling, it would be worth it, because he would get to spend time with Rachel.

Christmas turned him sappy, apparently. Who knew?

The queue shuffled up along the street as the doors to the store were opened. 'I don't see your stepsisters in this queue,' he said as they moved with the tide.

'They'll be inside already,' Rachel replied, absently. 'They're family.'

'So are you,' he pointed out, but she just

shrugged. He frowned. Seemed to him Rachel spent a lot of time not making a fuss about her awful family even when she really should.

Maybe he could help her start.

Finally they reached the front where the big double doors were propped open. Just inside, Rachel's father, stepmother and stepsisters were standing to receive their guests, handing each an envelope that Damon sincerely hoped contained a decent Christmas bonus for staff members.

'Rachel! You came! We weren't sure, after the dress debacle…' Maisie trailed off as Damon stepped out of the shadows behind his date and into full sight. 'And you brought a guest!' She elbowed her sister in the ribs and Gretchen turned to join them instantly.

'Oh, Damon, how kind of you to accompany Rachel *again*!' Gretchen simpered, making every hackle Damon possessed rise up. Whatever hackles were.

'I couldn't let my girlfriend attend her Christmas party alone,' he said, coolly. 'What kind of boyfriend would that make me?'

Both Gretchen's and Maisie's eyebrows shot up in symmetrical surprise.

'Boyfriend?' Maisie echoed. Then the stepsisters exchanged a knowing look. 'Oh, of course. Boyfriend. Just like Tobias was your boyfriend, I suppose? Well. Come on in, then!' She handed

Rachel her envelope. 'Enjoy the party, you two… lovebirds!'

Damon could hear them snickering behind him the whole walk to the temporary cloakroom that had been set up in the foyer.

'What was that about?' Rachel was tense beside him, almost rigid inside her coat, but she sighed at his question.

'They think it's an act,' she said, sliding her coat from her shoulders.

Damon took a moment to admire Rachel in that curve-clinging dress he'd bought on a whim—was it really less than two weeks ago? It seemed longer, somehow. But she still looked as beautiful, and as tempting, as she had in it at the TV studios that night.

The last time—the first time—he'd kissed her properly, and the moment he'd started losing his mind.

He frowned as her words caught up with him. 'An act?' Handing their coats over to the cloakroom assistant and taking their ticket, he led her away towards the bar. 'What kind of an act?'

Rachel rolled her eyes. 'Isn't it obvious? They think you're here as a pity date, pretending to be interested in me just so I'm not embarrassed by coming to the party alone. Even though I've come on my own for the last seven years.'

Seven years. She hadn't had a date at Christmas

in seven years. And yet, all Damon could think about was who she'd brought seven years ago. Someone she cared about? Someone she loved?

He shook the thought away. Was this why she'd latched onto the idea of a pretend date when they'd been talking last night?

He ran back over her stepsister's words in his head. *Tobias.*

*'Just like Tobias was your boyfriend...'* That was what she'd said.

'Who's Tobias?' he asked as they approached the bar.

Rachel's steps faltered just for a moment, then she carried on walking. 'My sort-of ex-boyfriend.'

'Sort-of ex?' he repeated. 'How does a person have a sort-of ex-boyfriend? Surely you're dating or you're not.'

'You'd have thought, wouldn't you?' Rachel said, her voice too light and cheery. She didn't want to talk about this, obviously. But he had a feeling she needed to, so he pushed all the same.

'Rach. Tell me about Tobias and I'll buy you the biggest glass of wine they sell here.'

She sighed. 'The glasses are all the same size— and the wine will be warm and you'll hate it. Besides, I have our drinks vouchers right here.' She waved the envelope he'd optimistically hoped, on behalf of the staff, would contain something more than a voucher for warm white wine.

'Then tell me because I want to know. And because I think you'll feel better for telling me.'

She gave him a disbelieving look at that. He waited and she eventually started to talk.

'Tobias was—is—a friend of Gretchen and Maisie. The same social circle, you know. We met by accident at one of the parties they threw at the house once, a year or so ago now, when Hannah and Dad were away. I normally try to stay out of the way when they're happening; I mean, I'm six years older than Maisie, and four years older than Gretchen, and we don't exactly have the same interests and friends, right?'

'I wouldn't imagine so,' Damon said, dryly.

'But that night they'd ordered the really good pizza, and I was starving, so I popped down. And Tobias…well, he seemed kind of on the outside too. So we got talking, and we actually got on well.'

'So far, so good. Why do I suspect this is all going to go wrong?'

'Because you've met me?' she guessed.

'I am one hundred per cent sure that whatever happened next is not your fault.'

'No, I guess not,' she admitted. 'Except for the part where I really should have known better.'

'What happened?'

'Long story short? We grew close. We were together for months. Except he was very, very careful to make sure that my stepsisters and their friends never saw us together. Which was easy, since I was never all that keen to be around them anyway. So much so, in fact, that it took me a while to notice.' She shook her head. 'I was naive. I should have realised sooner.'

'Realised what, exactly?' Damon could already feel the blood pounding at his temple. Just as well for this *Tobias* that he wasn't here tonight.

'That he was embarrassed to be seen with me.' Rachel shrugged, smiled a self-deprecating smile, and apparently remained unaware how much he wanted to punch her ex-boyfriend. Which was probably for the best. 'When we finally got caught out last summer—Gretchen, Maisie and a whole gang of friends walked in on us kissing—he laughed it off. Pretended it was all a big joke. That seducing me had been a sort of fun pastime, something to laugh about with his friends afterwards.'

Okay, now his blood really was boiling. 'That utter, utter bastard.' He wanted to touch her, to hold her, but he was too tense with anger.

Rachel, strangely, didn't look angry at all. Just said, 'I felt sorry for him, to be honest.'

At those words, his anger started to ebb away. 'Sorry for him?'

'Yeah. I mean, he cared more about what Gretchen and Maisie and everyone thought of him than what he actually wanted. And in some ways, he did me a favour.'

Okay, pity for the guy he could *almost* understand. But a favour? His scepticism must have shown on his face because she went on, unbidden.

'I mean, he showed me how small my life had become, stuck in that house, with those people. I've let them define me and my dreams for too long. Seeing Tobias choose their image of him over who he really was…that was what made me decide to finally stop doing that. To move out, find a new job, chase my own dreams for a change.' She sounded so strident, so determined, that Damon was almost fired up on her behalf.

Except that six months later she was still living there, still working at Hartbury's. 'What happened?'

Rachel's voice was small as she answered. 'Dad had a heart attack. He hadn't been feeling right for years—that was what always stopped me before. And then Hannah pointed out that me rowing with Gretchen and Maisie hadn't helped his stress levels. Might even have caused… Anyway. I just… I couldn't leave until I knew he was okay. We're just waiting on some last test results…'

'But you took the job at the arcade with me anyway.'

She looked up, her gaze locking onto his. 'It was too good an opportunity to pass up.'

The longer he held her gaze, the more he believed that she was saying something else. That *he'd* been the draw, not the job.

Then she looked away. 'Anyway, that's what happened. And that's why my stepsisters were so amused to see you with me. They think it's all pretend—a pity date or something.'

Because they didn't believe that any man would choose Rachel over them. Idiots.

'We're just going to have to show them this is no pity date, then, aren't we?' He couldn't change the heartbreak she'd felt last summer; he couldn't promise her anything beyond Christmas, either. But he could do this.

Rachel blinked up at him. 'And how, exactly, do you plan to do that?'

He felt the smile spreading across his face. 'Just trust me, yeah?'

She bit her lower lip, white teeth in plump flesh, and a shimmer of heat flashed through him. Proving this wasn't fake wasn't going to be a problem at all, not with the way he felt about Rachel in that dress.

'Okay,' she said.

And the game was on.

# CHAPTER TEN

THE HARTBURY'S CHRISTMAS party was as awful as it always was, objectively speaking. As always, they had tiny drinks vouchers in the envelopes provided at the door, ready to be exchanged for warm, weak wine and nothing else. As always, it was filled with people who already spent all day in each other's company, and really just wanted to get drunk and not have to talk to each other any more.

Being there with Damon was a definite improvement, though. He was attentive and boyfriendy without going over the top. Rachel could feel Gretchen and Maisie—not to mention plenty of others in the room—watching them as Damon led her onto the dance floor, or fetched her drinks, or just kept one hand casually at her waist as they spoke with other employees.

In fact, she even managed to relax in a way she'd never expected to. Until she spotted her stepmother crossing the room towards them, and saw the moment Hannah realised Rachel wasn't wearing the dress she'd bought her. She wouldn't have noticed when they arrived, not while she still had her coat on. But now there was no hiding it.

'Here we go…' she murmured.

Damon, handing her a glass of lukewarm wine, followed her gaze. 'Your stepmother?'

Rachel nodded. 'I'm not wearing the dress she bought for me.'

'I imagine because it was hideous?'

'Basically.'

'Okay, then.' Beside her, she felt him straighten his posture, and saw him paste on his most charming smile. *Battle armour*, she thought, wondering why she'd never noticed how often he used his charm as a defence before.

She tried to smile too, but it was hard in the face of Hannah's frown. 'Rachel, I think someone has caused some…unfortunate damage to one of the windows. Can you clean it up?'

'I—' Rachel started, glad that Hannah seemed too preoccupied by whatever had happened to the window display to have noticed the dress, but Damon interrupted her.

'Ms Hartbury? So nice to meet you. I'm Damon Hunter, an old friend of Rachel's.' The smile he shot her way as he said it made Rachel blush and caused Hannah to pause and turn her full attention to him instead.

'How nice of you to accompany her tonight,' she said, with the same scepticism her daughters had shown. 'I wasn't aware Rachel was bringing anybody.'

'It was kind of a last-minute thing,' she said hurriedly, drawing Hannah's attention back to her. Which was a mistake.

'You're not wearing the dress I bought you.'

'Oh, well. Um…you see…' Rachel tripped over her words, trying to find the ones that might appease her stepmother.

'That's my fault, I'm afraid, Ms Hartbury.' Damon's voice was smooth, but not exactly apologetic. 'I saw this one in your shop and couldn't resist buying it for Rachel. Don't you think it's just perfect for her?'

The way Hannah's gaze zipped up, down and back up again over Rachel's outfit, she suspected her stepmother thought the exact opposite. Neat and slim, like her daughters, Hannah had always frowned about Rachel's curves, as if the body shape she'd been born with—the one she had inherited from her mother—was something to be ashamed of. Embarrassed of, even by association.

Damon *liked* her curves, though. He'd bought her this dress to show them off before they'd ever even kissed.

That thought made Rachel stand a little straighter and smile a little more. 'It's very "me", don't you think?'

'I suppose,' Hannah said, doubtfully.

*'Is this thing on?'*

Rachel jumped at the sound of her father's voice, coming across the PA system. Turning, she found him standing half in one of the windows, talking into the microphone.

As the rest of the partygoers turned their attention on him too, he smiled and stepped down, holding the microphone out for Hannah, who was already striding towards him.

'What now?' Damon whispered.

'This is Hannah's traditional motivational speech for the workers.' Rachel patted his arm. 'It's about as awful as it sounds.'

As always, Hannah stood up at the front of the store, half on top of Rachel's window display, and made a horrible speech about teamwork and the shop being like a family—even though all the seasonal workers would be unemployed again in a couple of weeks. Rachel held onto her warm wine and willed it to be over.

Of course, then Hannah dragged Rachel's father and Gretchen and Maisie up front while she talked, speaking about the whole family being a team together too. Rachel was perfectly used to being left out of that sort of thing—and happier, to be honest—but she felt Damon tense beside her as Hannah threw out a casual mention of her existence.

'Oh, and thank you to my stepdaughter, Rachel,

of course, for her work on the window displays again this year.'

Nobody turned to find her. Nobody clapped. But then, Rachel hadn't expected them to.

Hannah was about to move on to the next part of her talk, the part traditionally dealing with expected behaviour at the party—no vomiting in the display mannequins—when a sound cracked through the room. Two hands, clapping.

Damon's hands.

He was applauding *her*. Her window displays. In a way that no one else would have even thought to.

Rachel could feel the heat flooding her cheeks, the embarrassment of being the centre of attention in a family and in a place where she was always an afterthought. She'd never wanted this, never wanted to be looked at, to be noticed, even.

But now it was Damon doing the looking, the noticing…and it turned out she didn't mind it half as much as she'd imagined she would.

Of course, when one person started clapping, human nature dictated that others would follow. And soon the whole room was applauding her little windows—even her stepsisters, for all they looked as if they'd rather be having their fingernails pulled out.

It was too much. Rachel twisted towards Damon to tell him to stop, but the thing had a momentum beyond him. He pulled her into his body, pressing a kiss to the top of her head, and she just knew everyone was watching.

'Look at me,' he murmured, and she couldn't help but obey. She met his gaze with her own, and had only a moment to recognise the warmth there before his lips lowered to hers.

She was kissing Damon Hunter. Again.

It shouldn't be such a surprise; they'd agreed to a fling, after all, hadn't they?

And yet…oh, and yet…

Rachel sank into the kiss, letting the world around them fall away as his tongue teased her lips. This wasn't a deep, passionate kiss, she realised—it was a show kiss, meant to show her family and colleagues that he was here as her real date tonight. That he wanted to be with her. That he liked her dress, her curves. That he liked *her*.

All the same, Damon's hands gripping her hips, holding her tight against him, and the small growl she heard from the back of his throat told her he wasn't *quite* as unaffected by this as he might pretend to be.

Good. If her entire self was melting and re-forming under his kiss, a growl was the least she could expect from him.

Someone, somewhere, maybe very far away, let out a whoop, breaking through the delicious bubble of solitude she and Damon had built around themselves. Then the real world began to leak in, starting with Hannah's voice over the PA system again, and Rachel pulled away from the kiss.

'Yes, well. Anyway, of course we want you all to enjoy yourselves tonight,' Rachel's stepmother said, somehow managing to make enjoyment sound like a punishable offence. 'But here at Hartbury's we do have certain standards to maintain.'

'I'm guessing we fail to meet the standard,' Damon whispered, and Rachel stifled a laugh. 'I think we proved our point, though. So... Want to get out of here?'

She did. Except the party was only halfway through. And she hadn't cleared up whatever mess was in one of the window displays. Could she really just walk out right now? In the middle of Hannah's speech?

'I didn't sort out the display,' she hedged, glancing towards the door.

Damon raised an eyebrow but didn't deign to answer that one. Instead, he ran his hand up over her hip, to her waist, then back down again. An innocent enough touch in public really, but one that shot through her body as if he'd been touching her somewhere else entirely.

And if she went home with him now, maybe he would.

Oh, hell. The cleaners would be in soon enough anyway. And it really wasn't her job…

'Let's go,' she said, and Damon smiled.

Somehow, it took both too long and too short a time to get back to his penthouse apartment. Damon had left the car in the secure garage under his building, figuring he might want a drink or two to get through the party, so they had to hail a black cab. They fell into the back of it together, Damon reluctant to let go of Rachel's hand even for a second, in case she slipped away.

Thankfully the driver wasn't the chatty type, but Damon found he couldn't make conversation with Rachel either. The tension, the chemistry between them, filled the cab until it was almost a visible fog. What could he say beyond 'I need to make love to you or I'm going to lose my mind'? Somehow he didn't think Rachel would appreciate him saying that in semi-public.

So yeah. He needed to get there quickly so he could say the words and, hopefully, follow through.

Which was the thought that made him think maybe he needed more time in the cab after all. Because this wasn't a one-night stand, wasn't a casual fling he was bringing home and would see for a few dates before they went their separate ways for ever.

This was Rachel.

And for all that she'd insisted that this *was* just a Christmas fling, and for all that he'd enthusiastically agreed to that, he hadn't considered how things would work after. Once things were over but they were still in each other's lives. They were friends, he hoped—through Celeste even if not in their own right. They were working together and he hoped that would continue past Christmas. The Cressingham Arcade would need social media support year-round, not to mention spring windows, summer windows, autumn windows... In fact, the odds were good that Rachel could be still working with the Arcadians, as he liked to call them, long after he'd moved on to his next project.

It was more than just that, though. More than friendship or working relationships. He *knew* Rachel. However determined she'd tried to sound suggesting the fling, her voice had wavered ever so slightly. This wasn't how she did things. Rachel Charles didn't have flings; she didn't fall into bed with just anybody. She was careful, especially after her past experiences. She'd chosen him and that meant he had to live up to her expectations. Not just in bed, but out of it too.

He couldn't hurt her; that was the first rule he'd set for himself. So he always had to be upfront about what he could give, and what he couldn't. So far, that had been easy enough.

But the next stage... Rachel wasn't good at speaking up, at asking for what she needed. He *knew* that. She was not used to being seen, or heard.

He saw her.

And he'd hear her, if she talked. But what if she didn't? What if she didn't tell him what she needed and he wasn't good enough to guess? He wanted her so badly that chasing his own pleasure was a necessity. But he wouldn't push her too far, ask for too much, or take her anywhere she wasn't comfortable.

So how did he make sure of that?

Rachel's hand landed hesitantly on his thigh and he looked up to see her chewing on her bottom lip.

'Okay?' His voice came out hoarse, embodying the strain on his whole self not to kiss her again right now.

'You looked like you were thinking hard,' she said, softly. 'I just wanted to say, if you've changed your mind...you know, about the whole Christmas-fling thing—'

'No!' Damon shouted, loud enough to make the silent taxi driver glance up at his mirror to check everything was okay. He tried to lower his voice as he carried on. 'Definitely not. Trust me. It is taking every bit of my self-control not to kiss you right now.'

'You could, you know,' Rachel replied, smiling prettily.

Damon shook his head. 'No. Because if I start kissing you, I won't be able to stop there.'

Her cheeks flared pink, even in the dark of the cab. 'Oh?'

'Yeah.' He met her gaze, letting all the wanting and the needing show in his eyes, and watched as her cheeks grew darker.

The cab stopped abruptly and, when Damon glanced out of the window, he saw they were at his flat. He still hadn't figured out exactly how any of this was going to work, but he knew one thing for sure: he was going to find a way to *make* it work.

No, *she* was. Because that was the answer, wasn't it? He had to surrender himself to what she needed.

He could do that.

Tossing some notes at the driver, and not waiting for any change, he opened the door and drew Rachel out behind him.

'Before we go up,' he said as they stood on the pavement, 'I want one thing to be very clear. You're in charge here, okay?'

She blinked at him. 'Um…okay? I don't really…'

'Once we get into that flat, nothing happens that you don't ask for. You can have basically anything you want, within reason. But you have to ask for it. Okay?'

He watched the war behind her eyes, the conflict of wanting what he was offering, and having to go against her own nature to get it.

But Damon knew that you only got what you asked for in this world. And if she wanted him, Rachel was going to have to learn to ask.

Damon's flat was everything she'd expected: expensive, stylish and soulless. At least, that was as much as she could tell from her brief glimpse around it as she stumbled through the door. After that, all she could focus on was Damon himself. Decor could wait.

'So…?' Damon stood before her, a wicked smile on his face. Her back was against the front door, the wooden frame something solid in a world that seemed to be shifting under her feet.

There was too much space between them, she realised, watching him. He was holding back, staying away. Waiting.

Waiting for her.

*'Once we get into that flat, nothing happens that you don't ask for.'* That was what he'd said.

And now he was making good on that promise.

Rachel swallowed, her mouth suddenly dry. With want—yes, definitely. But with fear too.

Asking for what she wanted sounded like such a simple thing to do. After all, she knew *exactly* what she wanted from Damon. She'd been fantasising about it ever since their kiss at the fake

New Year's Eve party. She'd imagined every single way he would touch her, kiss her, make love to her.

Knowing what she wanted wasn't the problem—in fact, it rarely was, in her life. She *knew*. She was just…oh, hell, she was scared to want it.

Scared to ask, in case the person who could give it to her said no. Scared to admit how *much* she wanted of the world, in case the world laughed in her face and asked her who she thought she was to demand such things. Just as it had when she'd asked the universe to save her mother. Or when she'd asked Tobias to love her, just as she was.

Scared of her own desires. Scared of screwing it up. Scared of a broken heart, further down the line.

The world was a terrifying place outside her bubble and outside the tiny perfect realities she created in her windows. Asking for more than she had, well, that had always seemed like rudeness. Entitlement. As her stepmother had told her often enough, she was lucky to have a nice home, a job, a family who accepted her, after her own mother had died. She was lucky. She still had her dad, at least.

What right did she have to ask for more?

And the last time she *had* asked, the last time she'd believed she deserved more love and affection than she was given…well, that had led to the whole debacle with Tobias. Was it any wonder she was scared to ask for more than her little life already gave her?

But she had, she realised suddenly. She'd *already* asked for more. Already stepped outside her bubble into the world of the Cressingham Arcade. She'd asked to change her shifts and the world hadn't ended. She'd taken Damon to the Christmas party, worn the wrong dress and, snide comments from her stepsisters aside, nothing terrible had happened. In fact, quite the opposite.

She'd asked Damon for a Christmas fling and he'd said *yes*.

'Rachel?' he asked now, a worried frown creasing his brow. She'd been thinking too long. Years too long, perhaps.

Now it was time to speak.

'I want you to kiss me,' she said, proud that her voice barely wavered at all.

Damon's frown disappeared into a warm smile and he stepped closer, his hands moving to her waist as if they belonged there. Maybe they did.

'Like this?' He pressed his lips to hers almost chastely, then pulled back.

She swallowed. 'No. Like this.'

Resting her palms against his shoulders, and hoping they weren't too sweaty, she stepped up into his space, until she could feel him sucking in a breath at her closeness. His whole ribcage moved, and, boy, did she love that she could affect him that way.

The power rush gave her the confidence to continue, reaching up on tiptoes and kissing him. There was nothing chaste about what she wanted from him, or about the kiss. The moment their lips touched, she felt the heat between them ignite and there was no holding back any more. It was as if, having decided to give in, her body was going to take full advantage of the opportunity and go for everything.

And despite Damon's obvious determination to let her lead the way, she could tell he was barely holding back from taking everything he wanted too.

Well, she wanted him to take it.

Breaking away, reluctantly, she tried to catch her breath—gratified to see that he was panting too.

'Too much?' he asked.

She shook her head. 'Not enough. Bedroom. Now.'

Rachel knew what she wanted. And she was ready to ask for it.

# CHAPTER ELEVEN

RACHEL DIDN'T KNOW how many hours later it was. Damon's bedside clock had been sacrificed to a particularly enthusiastic manoeuvre some time ago and her phone could, quite honestly, be anywhere. It didn't matter. Time had ceased to have any importance here in the cocoon of Damon's bedroom.

He'd made love to her with a thoroughness that shouldn't have been sexy, but really, really was. His attention to detail and focus in this particular area had been unsurpassed. But he'd been true to his word and had made her ask for every single step of it. She'd used words she hadn't previously even admitted to herself that she knew just to get where she needed to go.

And he had got her there. Twice.

'You okay?' Damon's voice was warm, private, and a little husky as he pulled her closer into his arms.

'More than.'

'Good.' He paused for a second, then asked, 'Do you need to get home tonight?'

She tried not to freeze but it was hard, even in

the warmth of his arms. *It's just a fling, Rach, remember? Maybe flings don't stay the night.*

She wouldn't know. She'd never had one before.

Suddenly, she felt as if she'd gone from having all the power to having none at all.

*Just ask.* Wasn't that what Damon had been showing her tonight? All the things that could be hers if she just asked for them?

She swallowed. 'Do you want me to go?'

His arms tightened around her. 'No. I'm hoping I can keep you here all night so we can do that again once I've recovered from the first round. I haven't even shown you my walk-in shower yet. I bet you can think of a few things to ask me to do in there.'

Her mind was already whirring with the possibilities while her body relaxed with the knowledge that he didn't want her to leave. 'I can stay.'

'Good.' He pressed a kiss to her curls. 'Your family won't miss you? I can probably track down your phone if you want to call them…'

Pulling back slightly, she raised her eyebrows and gave him a look of disbelief. 'You saw them tonight. Do you honestly think they're going to notice I'm not there?'

'Well, maybe not your stepsisters. Or your stepmother. Your dad?'

She shook her head. 'Probably not.'

That, of course, was the part that hurt the most.

Hannah, Gretchen and Maisie…they weren't blood family. They didn't choose her; she just came as a package deal. She could cope with them not caring.

But her dad… He loved her, she knew that. Every bit as much as she loved him. But he was torn between his love for her and his new family.

'He, well…when my mum died, he was an absolute wreck. People started telling him he had to pull it together for my sake. That I needed a family. A new mum, even. So he remarried to give me that. But instead, Hannah and the girls became his new family.' The memories hurt. She swallowed and forced herself to continue. 'He desperately wanted me to fit in with that too, to start with. He'd talk about how we'd be a proper family again, now we were all together, instead of it just being the two of us.'

'And you? Did you want that "proper family"?' It was as if now he'd touched her so intimately, seen every bit of her on the outside, he'd gained the ability to see inside too. Into her mind, into her heart.

She'd have to be careful with that. She knew what happened when people saw too deeply.

'No. I didn't.' She shifted just a little away from him. Still close, still in his arms, but not quite so intimate. 'I was happier when it was just the two of us. Mum…she died when I was twelve. I was old enough to remember what a real family felt like. And this…it wasn't that. Suddenly there were three other people and we lived in a new house—a bigger, better house, as Dad kept pointing out. But for me… I never felt like I was a part of it. I was fourteen when he remarried, raging at the world and, well, I guess I stopped trying to fit in at all.'

Would she have had a better relationship with her stepfamily if she'd made more of an effort to be part of it? Perhaps. But she knew herself too well now to believe that she could ever have been the sort of person that Hannah and her daughters valued. She would always have been lesser—less important, less beautiful, less rich. At least this way she got to be less on her own terms.

And right now, here in bed with Damon, she didn't feel less at all. She felt mighty.

'What about you?' she asked, suddenly keen to turn the conversation away from herself. 'I remember, when you used to come and visit us at university…'

'I'd get drunk and rant about my parents?' Damon finished for her, then sighed. 'Yeah, well. All teenagers do that.'

'True.' But somehow, she'd always suspected it was more than that with Damon and Celeste's family. The siblings were so different in so many ways, but Rachel had watched them closely enough to find the similarities too.

'My parents are…academics. Which isn't a bad thing. Except sometimes it feels like that's all they are. That even as kids Celeste and I were more like experiments, more academic curiosities than children. They are intelligent people and they expected us to be the same. Celeste never let them down there; she was as focussed on an academic career as they were. But I knew pretty early on I wasn't going to make that cut.'

Rachel wasn't sure she believed that. 'You're an intelligent guy, Damon. If you wanted to be an academic like your parents—'

'Ah, but that's the thing. I really didn't.' Sighing, he rolled further onto his side to look her in the eye. 'I saw how single-minded it made them all. How they ignored the whole rest of existence outside their little bubble and… I didn't want to be that way. I wanted to explore the world, meet new people, do new things. I didn't want to be tied down to one career, one obsession, my whole life.'

'That makes sense,' Rachel admitted. 'I guess some people know from really young what they want to do and be. Then for others…it takes us a bit longer.'

'Yeah. My parents never really understood that. Or me.'

'I think that's their loss,' Rachel told him. 'So

is that why you work for yourself? Why you take a different sort of project every time?'

*Why you never date the same woman more than a handful of times?*

Damon shrugged. 'I like variety. In all things.'

She heard the hidden message, whether he meant her to or not. She was a novelty, something new and interesting to pass the Christmas season. Once it was over, so were they.

Just as she'd told him she wanted. Just as she still should want.

And she would.

She'd take what she needed from this thing with Damon, then move on. Explore the wider world of possibilities he'd opened up for her.

Figure out what she wanted and ask for it.

Starting now.

'So, speaking of variety...' She moved closer, her whole body pressed up against his. 'Tell me more about this shower of yours.'

Damon grinned. 'Better than that, I'll show you.'

It should have been awkward afterwards. It usually was. Certainly, mornings after, in Damon's experience, had never been less than mortifying.

More often than not he tried to avoid them happening altogether. He'd sneak out of women's beds and apartments late at night and head home.

If they came back to his and somehow ended up staying the night, which didn't happen often in the first place, he had a routine for the following morning. He'd get up early, shower and dress, and be ready to claim an early morning meeting when they finally roused. He'd leave them with coffee, breakfast, and occasionally plans to get together in another week or so. Once or twice he'd even followed through on the plans without cancelling.

The point was, waking up in his king-sized bed to the weak winter sun already fighting its way through the window, Rachel propped up on one elbow watching him, should have been awkward. Beyond awkward. Alarm bells should have been ringing. He should have been bounding out of bed and racing for the shower, ready to escape. His heart should have been pounding with fear that she'd read more into what had passed between them than was really there.

Instead, as he opened his eyes and she smiled down at him, he smiled back.

He checked in quickly with his body—pleasurably aching—his mind—quiet, for once—and even his heart—still beating. The world seemed…fine. Right, even.

'Good morning,' Rachel murmured.

'Very,' he replied, then kissed her.

And as one kiss turned to another, he decided

that perhaps he was overthinking this after all. Maybe he could just enjoy being with Rachel, letting her ask for what she wanted and needed for once in her life, then leave her in a better place once Christmas was over. A place where she believed in herself, and had the confidence to show that to others.

The fact that he got incredible sex and lots of time with the most fascinating woman he knew was just an added bonus. Right?

Because in one night together, he'd already opened up more than he had with anybody since… well, since the last time he talked all night with Rachel, nine years ago. And he felt as if he'd seen the real Rachel again too. The passionate, open woman hiding behind the shy and reserved exterior she showed the rest of the world. He felt as if he'd gone through the window, into the deeper world she concealed inside, and he didn't want to leave.

So he pushed aside the part of his mind that reminded him how much this had scared him last time he'd grown close to Rachel. This time was different.

This time, he had an exit strategy. He could enjoy this, just until Christmas was over.

Five days later—five blissful, sex-soaked days later—came the first real test of their fling.

The days in between had been filled with waking up with Rachel, having breakfast with Rachel, walking to work with Rachel, working at the arcade with Rachel, having dinner with Rachel, going to bed with Rachel, making love to Rachel…

But he couldn't think about that last part now. Couldn't risk today's companion reading his mind, like some sort of witch.

Because today he wasn't working with Rachel, or doing anything with Rachel.

Today, he was Christmas shopping with his sister.

Across a rack of historically patterned scarves in the British Museum shop, Celeste narrowed her eyes at him. 'What is going on with you today?'

'Nothing,' he lied.

One eyebrow raised sceptically, she checked her watch. 'Well, there's nothing for Mum here. Come on, let's try the bookshop.'

If they ended up in the museum bookshop they would never, ever leave. 'What about this scarf?' he asked, grabbing the first item that came to hand.

Celeste cast a cursory gaze over it, then shook her head. 'That pattern is generally accepted to be from the right era, I admit, but Mum's latest research suggests it might actually be later, so it'll only cause an argument between her and Dad. Come on. Bookshop.'

Damon blinked down at the apparently controversial scarf. It looked like a nice pattern to him. *And this is why I don't go shopping for our parents' presents on my own*, he reminded himself as he hurried to catch up with Celeste.

They'd instigated the annual shopping trip for their parents' Christmas presents five years ago after a particularly disastrous round of gifts from Damon one year. *He'd* thought the racing wind-up monks were hilarious, but apparently not according to the rest of the family. Similarly, the British History tie that turned out to have some dating errors on it. In his defence, he'd already tried things like spa vouchers his mother never remembered to use before they expired and experience gifts for his father that apparently he didn't want to experience. He'd been running out of ideas and, frankly, enthusiasm. Especially since Celeste always managed to find the perfect—and historically accurate—gift for them both.

Celeste had insisted that next year they'd go shopping together for joint gifts. She'd said it at the Christmas dinner table so he'd been able to see the matching looks of relief on their parents' faces.

Sometimes he didn't know why he bothered buying them anything at all.

The museum bookshop curled around the centre of the circular Great Court, filled with all sorts of literature from academic tomes to light-hearted romps through history. Celeste obviously bypassed all the books he thought looked vaguely entertaining and went instead to the more academic end of things, eventually settling on a large, coffee-table photo book of archaeological digs through the ages.

'This will do for Dad,' she said, turning decisively towards the till. 'He'll enjoy criticising the older techniques. Now, once I've paid for this you can buy me a coffee and tell me what's going on with you and Rachel. Then we can go to this arcade of yours and look for something for Mum.'

Damon winced. He knew that tone. That was Celeste's *no arguing* tone.

'I'll go and get in the queue for the coffees.' At least that would give him a chance to figure out what he was going to say.

He was walking around the Great Court heading for one of the coffee stations when he was distracted by something in the children's shop. A small felt mouse, dressed in Victorian costume, singing from a tiny carol book. Smiling to himself, he picked it up, examining the details and imagining Rachel's smile if she saw it.

He glanced back over his shoulder but there was no sign of his sister yet. Celeste was bound to get distracted by the books on her way to the till. He had time.

Decision made, he paid for the mouse, then continued to the café.

He might not be any good at shopping for his parents, but at least there was someone in the world he knew a good gift for when he saw it.

'So,' Celeste said, easing herself onto the bench across the table from him ten minutes later. He pushed her coffee towards her, hoping it might mellow her somehow. 'You and Rachel.'

'You've spoken to her?' He needed to know what she already knew before he could figure out his line of defence.

'No. That's how I know there's something going on. She's dodging my calls.'

Damon winced. 'Not dodging. She's…been busy.'

'With you.'

'Well, yes. We're working together.'

Celeste pinned him to his seat with her steeliest gaze. 'And is that all you're doing together?'

'Isn't this a conversation you should be having with your best friend?'

'I'm trying to have it with my brother. Damon, I warned you not to mess her around—'

'I'm not!'

'Oh, so this is true love at last?' Celeste scoffed.

'I didn't say that.'

'Of course not. You wouldn't ever. And Rachel *deserves* true love.'

*I know that.*

Worse, he knew he wasn't the person who could give it to her.

*'You have no focus, Damon. You can't commit to anything.'* His mother's voice was echoing Celeste's implications in his head.

Damon sighed. 'Look. If I promise you that I know what I'm doing, will you let this drop?'

She raised both eyebrows at that. Never a good sign. 'That depends. *Do* you know what you're doing?'

The lie was on the tip of his tongue. How hard was it to just say *yes*? To blithely promise that he had everything in hand and there was no need to worry, just as he did for work projects all the time? Even when things were a little off course, he always managed to bring them back round again. He'd do the same this time.

So he hadn't planned on a festive fling with his sister's best friend. But now he was there… he could hardly imagine this Christmas happening any other way.

*'Do you?'* Celeste pressed.

'I hope so,' Damon replied, and prayed that would be enough.

Rachel was just putting the finishing touches to the window of Jasmine's Bridal and Formal Wear

Boutique when she heard her best friend's voice behind her.

She froze, one hand still holding a small posy of holly, mistletoe and white roses she'd begged from Belinda the florist but had yet to find the perfect place for. If Celeste was here that meant Damon was probably back too, which was good because she hadn't seen him all day.

But if Celeste was here it was also bad. Because it probably meant she'd realised Rachel had been avoiding her all week.

Quickly, Rachel tucked the posy into the hands of a bridal mannequin dressed in an icy lace wedding dress—with tiny mice pulling tight the ribbons of her bodice—and ducked out of the window into the shop. Jasmine was still behind the counter, humming to herself as she worked. Rachel thought she was making a tiara, although she wasn't entirely sure. She also had bigger issues.

*'Avoiding you?'* she whispered to herself, practising the upcoming conversation under her breath. *'Why would I be avoiding you?'* She added a tiny laugh at the end, hoping it sounded genuine.

Behind the counter, Jasmine looked up, staring straight at her. 'If you're trying to sound convincing, you need a lot more practice than that.'

'No time,' Rachel said as the door to the shop swung open.

'There you are!' Celeste swept into the shop, elegant in her soft white woollen coat, her dark hair tucked up in the sort of clip Rachel's curls would escape from in a heartbeat. She wrapped one arm around Rachel in a perfunctory hug, the other arm weighed down by an enormous black handbag. Knowing Celeste as she did, it was probably full of reading material and notes rather than Christmas shopping.

'Hi, Celeste.' Rachel met Damon's gaze over his sister's shoulder. He had the beaten-down look of a man who knew he couldn't win the fight he was in.

People often had that look around Celeste. Normally she wouldn't read too much into it, except this time...this time, she was pretty sure the fight was about *her*.

'I thought you two were shopping at the British Museum today,' Rachel said, stepping back. She held her hands clasped in front of her, trying desperately not to fidget. Celeste was her best friend, for heaven's sake. Why was she nervous now? Especially when she'd spent almost a whole week with Damon, learning *not* to be nervous about asking for what she needed.

She straightened her spine and looked over to see Damon giving her an approving smile.

'I wanted to see this arcade that's got you and Damon so busy this month,' Celeste said, glancing around the boutique. 'You know me, I'm not much of a shopper.' It was one of the things that had drawn Rachel and Celeste together at university when everyone else was spending their student loans on new clothes. 'But this place is stunning. I can see why you both love it. And your window displays are amazing.'

'That's why I had to have her. For this project, I mean,' Damon added hurriedly as Rachel's eyes widened. 'I knew she'd be perfect for the Cressingham Arcade.'

Celeste still had her back to her brother so he couldn't see her raising her eyebrows in an amused expression. But Rachel could. She'd had years of translating Celeste's every slight frown or eyebrow lift, every half-smile or concerned look. And Celeste could read hers too. Between them, they could have an entire conversation across a library and know when the other needed rescuing from an overenthusiastic fellow researcher. It also worked well on their rare nights out in pubs and clubs. It was how Rachel had known that her friend was overcompensating for nerves as she argued with Theo at the filming.

And right now, she knew Celeste was saying, *He thinks he's so subtle, but he really isn't.*

She smiled in agreement, and Celeste's expression changed—a slight furrowing of the brow, a small, sideways half-smile, concern in her eyes.

*Are you okay? With everything? Do I need to beat up my brother? Because I will.*

Rachel knew it. But there was no need.

Damon had been perfect all week. Alarmingly so, in fact. She'd expected him to freak out when they woke up together on Saturday morning, but he hadn't. In fact, he'd been so okay with it that they'd barely been apart since. She'd actually been the one who was unsure about that, suggesting that maybe she should go home at least *sometimes*. But Damon had asked her why she'd want to and she hadn't been able to think of a good reason so she'd stopped by the Hartbury family home long enough to pack a bag and that was about it. She wasn't sure if her family had noticed.

The thing was, she reasoned to herself in the dark of the night, she only had this Christmas with Damon. A festive fling, that was all.

So she might as well make the most of every minute of it.

Celeste was still watching her, waiting for her response, that furrow of a frown line growing deeper with each passing second. Rachel wondered what Damon had told her. She'd have to ask him later. But for now, she needed to reassure her best friend that she knew what she was doing, that she wasn't about to get her heart broken. Probably.

So she smiled, eyebrows neutral, gave a slight nod and watched Celeste relax. Mission accomplished.

Celeste clapped her hands together as if they'd had an actual conversation, instead of a weird eyebrow discussion. 'Great! Well, in that case, Damon, I assume you're bringing Rachel to the traditional Hunter Christmas Eve party this year?'

Damon, understandably, looked a little lost at the sudden change of topic. 'Uh, we hadn't talked about it. But, if you'd like to come… I'd love to have you there.'

She hadn't had as many years translating Damon's expressions and hidden words but, after the last week, she liked to think she was getting better. So she heard the truth in his words and hoped she understood them.

He didn't want to go to the family party, she knew that. But if he had to be there, he'd rather be there with her at his side. And that felt pretty wonderful. It felt like…hope.

'Okay,' she whispered, and watched the smile spread across his face.

'In that case, you're going to need something to wear.' Celeste spun slowly around, taking in all the beautiful evening dresses and wedding gowns the boutique racks held. 'I'm fairly sure you can find the perfect dress here, don't you think?' She smiled at Jasmine, who darted out from behind the counter and grinned as she sized Rachel up.

'We absolutely can,' she promised. 'I'm thinking something red. The colour of a really good red wine.'

'My favourite,' Damon said, moving behind Rachel. He lowered his voice so only she could hear. 'I'm thinking something that slides off your shoulders all the way to the floor the minute we get home again.'

Her cheeks warmed at that, but Celeste didn't seem to notice.

'Perfect,' she said, and turned to them both. 'And after that, we need to go out for lunch, so you can both meet my sort-of date for the party too.'

Rachel and Damon exchanged a look, one that Celeste could probably have read effortlessly if she hadn't already been looking through dresses with Jasmine with more enthusiasm than Celeste had ever shown about anyone's wardrobe, including her own, previously.

Celeste had a *date*?

# CHAPTER TWELVE

CELESTE HAD SPENT all morning grilling him about his relationship with Rachel, and now this? She'd avoided all of his questions under the premise of concentrating on choosing the perfect dress for Rachel—which they had—and then been tight-lipped all the way in the cab to the restaurant she, or rather her date, had apparently booked for the four of them.

'Do you have any idea who she's been seeing?' he murmured to Rachel as Celeste paid the driver.

She shrugged. 'None. To be honest, I haven't been paying a lot of attention to the world outside the Cressingham Arcade for the last week.'

'Apart from the world inside my apartment,' he pointed out, mostly just to watch the pink spread across her cheeks as she remembered all the places in that apartment he'd kissed, touched and made love to her over the last five days.

She gave him a secret smile, one he'd come to know and adore since they began their festive fling. He returned it, then looked up to find Celeste watching them, her expression speculative. Damn.

He really didn't need her getting ideas that this was anything more than he'd told her it was, more than he and Rachel had *agreed* it was.

Well, he thought as Celeste swept into the restaurant, this lunch would have to be his chance to convince her of the truth. And tease her mercilessly about keeping her new boyfriend from them. Not enough to scare the poor guy off—although, if he was dating Celeste, he had to have a higher tolerance for terror than most men anyway. It would probably take a lot more than an amused little brother to ruin things.

Then he saw Theo Montgomery sitting alone at a table for four and realised that this double date was going to be even more bizarre than he'd imagined.

'Is that…?' Rachel trailed off, her mouth still slightly open with astonishment.

'Apparently. Something you want to tell us, Celeste?'

'Just…pretend this is all totally normal, okay?' His sister straightened her spine, pasted on a smile and led them across the restaurant to Theo's table.

Damon watched in astonishment as Theo stood, smiling, and embraced Celeste, kissing her right on the lips. And Celeste, against all possible odds, returned the kiss, blushing prettily as she stepped away afterwards.

Was he in another dimension? It seemed possible. And more likely than Celeste and Theo actually being in love and not bickering with each other.

'Sweetheart, you remember my brother, Damon? And his girlfriend, Rachel?'

Okay, Celeste had definitely never called anyone 'sweetheart' in her life. Something was definitely going on here— Wait. Did she call Rachel his girlfriend?

It was too late to correct her now, he supposed, while Theo was hugging Rachel in welcome, and holding out a hand for him to shake. Damon took it then moved closer to the table, pulling out Rachel's chair first instinctively, only realising he'd done it when he saw Theo doing the same for Celeste.

What followed had to be the most surreal meal of his life, and he said that as someone who had experienced his father's attempts to recreate an Ancient Roman banquet, complete with honeyed dormouse. Watching Theo and Celeste be not just civil, but actually affectionate with each other, to the point of Theo feeding her some of his starter from his own fork, was just baffling. As far as he could tell, Rachel was equally confused, although she managed to keep up something of a conversation with Celeste.

Damon tried to chat with Theo but, to be honest, his mind was occupied by other things. Like Celeste calling Rachel his girlfriend.

Girlfriend implied long term—certainly past Christmas. It implied deeper feelings than Damon was willing to commit to. And worse than that, it gave people—namely Rachel—ideas.

He needed to talk to his sister, make the situation even clearer than he had over coffee that morning. Hadn't she been the one who'd pointed out that Rachel deserved more than him? So why was she suddenly pushing like this, inviting Rachel to the family party, calling her his girlfriend?

Although having Rachel at his parents' Christmas Eve party with him was the only thing that could make the night bearable, as far as he was concerned.

Still. It wouldn't do for anyone to get ideas, that was all. Especially not him.

It wasn't until the puddings were eaten that Theo suddenly sat up straighter, leaning around Celeste to watch something out of the window, then collapsed back into his seat with obvious relief.

'He's gone?' Celeste asked, shifting her chair away from Theo's to a more normal distance.

Theo nodded. 'Finally.'

Beside Damon, Rachel frowned. 'Who's gone?'

'Our reporter stalker,' Theo said, with a tired

smile. 'Come on, let's grab after-lunch drinks in the back bar where it's more private. Then we can explain.'

The back bar was cosy, warm and empty. Theo spoke briefly to the head waiter on their way in and he nodded, then shut the door behind them, returning moments later to enter, after knocking, with a tray of coffees and liquors. Then he departed again, leaving them in peace.

It didn't escape Rachel's notice that, now they no longer had an audience, Celeste and Theo were sitting as far away from each other as they could manage while still at the same table.

Damon had noticed too. He looked between them once, twice, then just asked. 'What the hell is going on here?'

Rachel let out a breath and took a seat—one next to Celeste, just in case her friend needed her. She hadn't seen any hint of this, whatever *this* was, in Celeste's manner when they'd been dress shopping at the arcade. And surely if something really weird was going on Celeste would have told her?

*When?* her mind asked rebelliously. *When you were avoiding her calls because you were in bed with her brother and you knew she wouldn't approve?*

Okay, fine. She'd been a rubbish friend this

month. But now she was here, she was every bit as curious as Damon as to what was going on.

'Do you want to explain, or shall I?' Theo asked Celeste, his upper-class tone lazy.

'I'll do it,' Celeste replied, sharply. 'You'll get it wrong.'

'Probably,' Theo agreed easily. 'I'll pour the coffees, then.'

'So, Damon, I know you watched the car crash that was our festive TV quiz. Rachel, I assume you did too?' Celeste asked.

Rachel nodded, although in truth she'd only been able to bear watching the highlights on the Internet after the event. They were definitely bad enough.

'It didn't go down particularly well with the Internet fans. Or my agent,' Theo said.

Celeste shot him a look that Rachel interpreted as, *Who is telling this story, you or me?* Theo had obviously spent enough time with Celeste to read it too as he shut up and let her continue.

'So Theo called me and asked me to help him rehabilitate his reputation.'

'And yours,' Theo interjected.

Celeste rolled her eyes. 'My reputation is based on my research, my publications, my education and my brain, not my ability to be pleasant on television. Unlike yours.'

'Your reputation with TV companies, however,

is based *entirely* on that,' Theo pointed out, apparently unruffled by the accusation that he was just a pretty face.

Celeste ignored him.

Rachel snuck a look across the table at Damon, who was glowering at both of them. For all that he was the younger of the two siblings, she knew he could still be fiercely protective of his big sister. If he thought Theo was using Celeste…

'So what happened next?' she asked, keen to move the conversation along before the two of them descended into bickering again.

'We agreed to a few public appearances together, as friends,' Celeste said, as if it were the most normal thing in the world. Maybe it was in *Theo's* world, but Rachel knew for a fact that Celeste had never once in her life pretended to be anything she wasn't.

And now she was pretending to be Theo's friend? Girlfriend, even?

'It got a little bit out of hand from there,' Theo admitted. 'There were these stories online…'

'People thought we were faking it,' Celeste explained.

'Which you were.' Damon, Rachel noticed, was still glowering as he spoke.

'So we had to prove that we really *were* okay with each other,' Celeste went on, ignoring her brother. 'By pretending we were in love.'

'So you're mortal enemies pretending to sleep together for the cameras,' Damon said, dryly. 'The miracle of modern love, huh?'

'Like you can talk,' Celeste scoffed, then turned to Theo. 'This one spent all morning telling me how he and Rachel are just colleagues who sleep together. Apparently they're having a "festive fling".'

Oh.

*Oh.*

There was nothing about the words that were untrue, Rachel knew that. It was exactly what they'd agreed—a festive fling, nothing serious. Just something that would make the time while they were working together more fun.

And yet, every syllable of Celeste's words seemed to slice off another section of her heart.

She knew she couldn't let it show. This was like Tobias all over again, even if it shouldn't be. Tobias had lied to her, let her believe that what he felt for her mattered to him. Damon had never done that. He wasn't hiding her away, he wasn't ashamed of his attraction to her. He liked her, wanted her, desired her, enjoyed her company. All of that was still true, and he'd never promised anything more. She couldn't hold this against him.

But she could still feel the other three watching her, waiting to see if she'd fall apart, as she had when she'd realised the truth about Tobias.

*Not this time.* This time she was stronger. This time, she knew she'd be okay.

Yes, she might have very stupidly fallen for a man who had told her upfront he wasn't in this for the long haul, but she'd told him the same. Now she just had to suck it up and deal with it.

Even if she was realising, rather too late, that she might be just a little bit in love with him.

Rachel forced herself to smile, just as Celeste said, 'Sorry, Rachel, that came out wrong.'

'No, it's true.' She reached for her liquor. That might help. 'He's my festive fling. Right, Damon?'

'Right.' But even he didn't look convinced.

She took a sip of her drink and reminded herself to keep breathing.

She'd figure this out. Find a way to save her battered heart.

But if she only had one more week with Damon Hunter before their Christmas romance was over, she wasn't going to waste any of it moping about. She was going to enjoy every second.

Four days after the double date from hell, the Cressingham Arcade officially opened to the public, not that it had been fully closed all along. But the scaffolding and cordons were gone, the floor tiles were repaired, the window displays were beautiful—apart from Mr Jenkins's jewellery shop, because the old codger had kept putting off letting Rachel in to arrange anything—and Rachel's social media campaign had built to such a frenzy that there were actual queues waiting outside the arcade at opening time.

'I can't believe we really did it,' Rachel said, her eyes wide with astonishment as Lady Cressingham formally opened the gates for the first time.

'I can,' Damon told her, but he was watching her, not the crowds.

She'd made this happen. He hoped she knew how incredible that made her.

He tried to show her, that night in bed. Tried to tell her how amazing she was. But that connection, the one he'd felt since the first time they kissed…it seemed closed off. As if he couldn't get through to her any more.

Was it because they were coming to the end of their time together? Probably. It made sense to try and pull away before they had to, to ease the ending. He should probably be trying to do the same thing.

But he couldn't. Because every time he thought about not waking up to Rachel's face smiling at him, he felt as if he couldn't breathe.

But he was going to have to figure it out, he resolved, in a stern pep talk to his reflection in the kitchen window of the Hunter family townhouse, three days later. Because tonight was Christmas Eve and, after tomorrow, their festive fling would be over. Which meant he'd have to spend the dying minutes of it here, in his parents' town house. His least favourite place in the world.

He fingered the felt mouse in his pocket, the one he'd bought at the British Museum. He hadn't found the right moment to give it to Rachel just yet, but he supposed he'd better find it tonight.

It might be his last chance.

'What are you brooding about in here?' Celeste asked, walking into the kitchen and catching him glaring at the drinks trolley.

'Who says I'm brooding?'

'Anyone who can see you.'

'Which is…' Damon looked ostentatiously around them '…basically just you.'

Grabbing a tea towel from the counter, Celeste swatted him lightly with it, the way she used to when they were kids. 'Is it Rachel?'

'Is what Rachel?'

That earned him an eye-roll. 'Is it Rachel that's making you so broody?'

'If I were brooding—and that's a big if,' he added as Celeste made her *I knew I was right* smug face. 'If I were, there would be no reason for it to be about Rachel.'

Except, of course, it was. And his sister wasn't

falling for any twisted non-answers he might give, unfortunately.

'So, which is it?' She hopped up onto the kitchen counter and ticked the options off on her fingers. 'You're bored of her already and regretting asking her to come tonight because it will end your chances of picking up someone else.'

'*No.*' Damon grabbed the ice tray from the freezer and started bashing the cubes out into the ice bucket, as his mother had asked him to before his broodfest had started.

'Okay, good, because I really would have snapped that towel at you if you had. Okay, option two: you're worried that she's falling in love with you, and you're going to hurt her when you end things *just like I said you would.*' The last part was loud enough that Damon half expected his parents to come rushing in to see what they were arguing about.

Except since they'd rarely ever done that when they were kids, it seemed unlikely they were going to start now. Not when they were each busy in their own private rooms, preparing for the party ahead.

'That's not the problem,' he said, curtly. 'Now, if you don't mind, I've got a list of tasks to finish before Mum comes down—' Damon tried to move towards the door, but Celeste swung her long legs up to rest on the counter opposite, blocking his way out of the narrow galley kitchen.

'In that case, that only leaves option three.'

'Which is?' he asked impatiently, even though he didn't really want to know.

'That you don't want to end it at all. That you've fallen for her. Properly.' There was a hint of awe in Celeste's voice at the very possibility.

'Don't be ridiculous,' he said, even though his heart was beating too fast at her words.

'I don't think it's ridiculous. I mean, Rachel is far too good for you, but other than that—'

He pushed her legs out of the way and stepped through. As if he didn't already know that. 'Unless you and Theo are going to come clean tonight that your whole relationship is a lie—or announce that you're actually madly in love and planning the wedding—please stop lecturing me about my situation with Rachel, okay?'

She bristled at the mention of Theo, just as he'd known she would, and he escaped without further comment from her. Their whole lives, the easiest way to distract Celeste had always been to bring up her own shortcomings.

It made a change from thinking about his anyway.

# CHAPTER THIRTEEN

CHRISTMAS EVE. HOW was it Christmas Eve already?

The last week had seemed to go both too fast and too slow for Rachel. Every day was so busy, between the opening of the arcade, her shifts at Hartbury's, and spending her evenings and mornings with Damon, the time had flown by. Counting down to the moment her life went back to normal, the way it had been before Damon Hunter had swept her onto a dance floor at fake midnight and kissed her.

And yet, at the same time…every moment she'd spent with Damon had seemed to last longer. Maybe because she was so determined to remember every last second. Or perhaps just because she could already feel the distance growing between them.

Now, as she finished up her last shift at Hartbury's before it closed for Christmas, she wondered how, exactly, she'd be able to go back to that old life. She wasn't the person she'd been then. How could she be, when she'd lived a whole life's worth of missed romance and seduction in less than a month?

The bell had rung to announce closing time almost fifteen minutes earlier and the children's-wear floor she was covering that afternoon was empty. Time to get ready for Damon and Celeste's parents' party—and to say goodbye to her festive fling for good. Just until Christmas, that was what they'd decided—what she'd insisted on. And now Christmas was here.

At least she was going to see it out in style. Grabbing the bag she'd brought from her little closet office, she headed for the changing rooms to get ready for the party. It didn't take long to wriggle into the silky, wine-red dress she'd chosen from Jasmine's collection, although she decided to save the high heels until she'd found a taxi, just in case. Her dark curls didn't need much more than a fluff—they were going to do whatever they wanted anyway so she might as well just let them get on with it.

She was halfway through putting her make-up on when she realised she was no longer alone.

'Another party, Rachie?' Gretchen asked. Rachel spun to find both her stepsisters watching her from the doorway to the fitting room. 'You're getting to be quite the party animal, aren't you?'

'Compared to who?' Rachel asked, without

thinking. But really, she'd been to two parties that month, and one of those was the shop one.

Maisie's smile twisted a little, making her beautiful face a little uglier. 'We're just worried about you, Rachie. Don't think we haven't noticed you staying out until all hours—or worse, not coming home at all.'

'You don't need to worry about me,' Rachel said, stiffly. How could she have believed they wouldn't notice? Of course they would. Mostly to give them ammunition to cause trouble for her later.

'But we *do*! You're our sister after all.' Gretchen swept into the changing room, casting an eye over Rachel's outfit. Rachel fought the urge to scream *step*sister at her.

'It's Damon, isn't it?' Maisie followed her sister, as always, until between them they were almost surrounding her, blocking her between the mirrored walls and themselves. 'You're falling for him.'

'And that worries us too,' Gretchen added. 'You're so naive when it comes to love, Rachie.'

'Remember Tobias?' Maisie added, as if Rachel were *ever* likely to forget that particularly humiliating episode.

'We just don't want something like that to happen to you again, is all.' Gretchen reached out to touch the silky fabric of her dress and Rachel flinched away. 'I mean, dressing up to try and impress him? It's just not you, Rachel.'

'You know he's using you, right?' Maisie said, bluntly. 'I mean, why else would he be interested? He's got you working over at that arcade everyone's talking about, hasn't he? I've seen the social media campaign.'

'Luckily for you, I don't think Mum has.' Gretchen raised an eyebrow as she spoke. 'And of course *we* wouldn't show her.'

*Yes, you would*, Rachel thought. *Why haven't you?*

Maisie shot an irritated look at her sister. That was unusual too; they were always so in sync.

'The point is, now the place is open he won't need you any more, Rachel. And we don't want you going out there embarrassing yourself again, like before.' Maisie's gaze was wide and guileless and Rachel didn't buy it for a minute.

Unwilling to look either of them in the eye a moment longer, Rachel found herself staring at her own reflection, along with her stepsisters'. The two of them loomed over her in their heels, their immaculate outfits, hair and make-up as intimidating to her as always.

For just a second, she let it get to her.

Were they right? Had the festive fling just been a convenient way to keep her onside while they worked on the project?

*Just colleagues who sleep together.*

No. She knew it was more than that because she'd seen the passion in Damon's eyes when he watched her, felt his need for her in his touch. She'd laughed with him, talked with him, relaxed with him—and felt more herself than she had done in years, just from being in his presence.

With Damon, she'd found the courage to ask for what she needed—and now she hoped she'd continue to have that strength without him.

Because Gretchen and Maisie were right about one thing. After tonight, it was all over between them.

*Unless it isn't.*

The possibility welled up in her too fast, too strong for her fear to stamp it down.

Because she *knew* Damon wasn't giving up on them for any of the reasons her stepsisters were suggesting. Their fling was ending because that was what she'd asked for. And if she wanted something different now...

Well. She had to ask for that too.

*He might say no.*

She felt the truth settle in her heart, and knew there was a very good chance he would. Damon Hunter didn't settle down, didn't choose one path if it closed off all the others. He liked to keep his options open and what she wanted from him was the opposite of that.

She didn't want a festive fling.

She wanted Damon forever. Hers.

Which meant she had to tell him that. Tonight.

Spinning around, she grabbed her bag and figured she'd sort out her make-up in the taxi using her phone camera.

'Where are you going?' Gretchen called after her.

'Didn't you listen to anything we said?' Maisie yelled.

Rachel turned and walked backwards for a few steps as she replied, glad she hadn't put her heels on yet.

'I listened,' she said. 'And I know you're wrong. So, if you'll excuse me, I'm off to find my own life, for a change.'

Then she turned her back on them and headed for the doors.

His mother was complaining about something but Damon had tuned her out minutes ago. Or years ago, perhaps. All he knew was that there was something wrong with the ice—inexplicably, since surely ice was ice?—that Celeste was still glaring at him across the room, and that his father was deep in conversation with Theo Montgomery. Or, more accurately, his father was talking, at length, and Theo was listening politely.

Oh, and Rachel wasn't there yet. He was definitely aware of that.

'And I don't know *what* your father is finding to talk to *That Man* about,' his mother said as Damon tuned back in.

'I think *That Man* is just a convenient audience for Dad to practise his latest lecture.' Theo Montgomery had gone down about as badly as expected as a boyfriend for Celeste. It wasn't as though she'd brought many home before now, but Theo was definitely at the bottom of the list. He didn't even *have* a PhD.

His mother sniffed. 'I don't know what happened to that nice boy from the Philosophy department.'

'I think you and Dad scared him off after his first Sunday dinner,' Damon said mildly, safe in the knowledge that his mother wasn't listening to him anyway.

'At least he knew what he wanted, knew what *mattered* to him.' His mother gave him a sideways look. 'Which is more than we can say for some people.'

Yes, yes. Because he was hopelessly uncommitted. His parents' motto was practically, *If you don't know what matters to you, then you don't matter at all.* He was used to not mattering. It didn't bother him any more.

Where was Rachel? Tonight was the last night of their festive fling; that was the deal. And he didn't want to miss a moment of it. So where was she?

He scanned the room again in case he'd missed her, although he couldn't see how that was possible. But he did realise suddenly that his sister was missing. Which meant…

Turning his back on his mother—not that she noticed—he focussed on the door that led in from the main hallway to the living room and dining room, which had all been opened up for the party. Any moment now…

*There.*

Even though he'd been preparing himself for it all day, the sight of Rachel in that wine-red dress still took his breath away. Her hand tucked through Celeste's arm, she entered the room smiling and he could sense the other guests turning to look at her. Even with the dress she still looked just like the same Rachel he'd known for so long, her curls rioting around her head, her make-up minimal, her figure gorgeously curvaceous. But there was something new about her too. And that was what was making everyone stare, where before they might have overlooked her.

Damon wasn't conceited enough to believe that the difference was him, but it *was* visible. As she walked towards him, it clicked.

It was her confidence.

She wasn't looking at the ground, avoiding everyone's gaze. She wasn't clinging to the walls hoping no one noticed she was there, hoping no one asked her anything.

She had her head held high, a secret smile around her mouth—the smile of a woman who knew what she wanted and intended to get it. And she was heading straight for him.

Suddenly, the pain in his chest wasn't from lack of breath. It was pangs of fear. Because he knew that look; he'd seen it before on other women's faces. That was the smile of a woman who thought she had him where she wanted him. Who thought he couldn't possibly let her down now.

He'd let them all down, every one of them. Starting with his parents, then his sister, then every woman he'd ever dated, he'd let down every single person who'd ever looked at him that way. With expectation. Because that was what he did.

And as much as he might hate himself for it, he knew he was going to do the same thing to Rachel. Because that was just who he was. Damon Hunter, commitment-phobe, flake, unreliable guy.

Why on earth had he thought he could be anything different, even for a moment? That he could get out of this festive fling with everyone's heart and pride intact?

*You don't want to end it at all. You've fallen for her. Properly.*

Those weren't his words, weren't his thoughts. They were Celeste's. And if he'd never listened to his sister before, he wasn't going to start now.

He and Rachel had made an agreement: a festive fling. And he was sticking to it. That was all there was to it.

Maybe his decision showed on his face because as he straightened his spine and tried to smile, Rachel stumbled, just a little. Celeste caught her arm and he saw Rachel murmur something to her. His sister nodded then, Rachel steady again, and peeled off to head towards Theo. Damon stopped paying her any attention at that point.

He couldn't see anything but Rachel. And how everything good in his life was about to blow up in his face.

Oh, goodness, she wasn't sure if she could do this. Just the look on Damon's face as he watched her…he knew what was coming, she could tell. He was figuring out how to let her down gently.

Because what she was about to do wasn't what they'd agreed. It wasn't *fair*. And she was going to do it anyway, because it was a hell of a lot more honest and important than any agreement about a festive fling.

'You okay?' Celeste murmured as Rachel slipped, one of her high heels skidding on the Hunters' parquet flooring.

'No.' She grabbed onto Celeste a little tighter while she found her balance. 'But I will be.'

'Do you want me to come with you to talk to him?'

Because of course Celeste knew what she was going to say. She was transparent. The moment Celeste had opened the door she'd taken one look at her and said, *'Oh, my God, you're in love with my brother.'*

That was what happened when you only had one good friend your entire adult life. They could tell *everything*.

'No,' Rachel told her now. 'I need to do this alone.'

'You're sure?'

Rachel looked again at Damon. He looked as if he was steeling himself for a horrible scene. Maybe he was. She'd never had this kind of conversation before. Never had this kind of confidence before. She didn't know how it was going to go.

But she still wasn't strong enough to do this with too much of an audience.

'Sure. Besides, I need you to do something else for me.'

'Anything,' Celeste said.

'Distract the rest of the room?' The party wasn't so big that the small crowd would be able to ignore any argument between her and Damon. Apparently the Hunters' idea of a party was more like everyone else's idea of having a few friends round. Or maybe they just didn't have that many friends. 'Just while I get Damon out of here. I don't want an audience for this.'

Celeste shot her a crooked smile. 'On it.'

Rachel took another breath and continued on towards her doom.

Damon smiled as she reached him, obviously hoping he could pretend there was nothing unusual going on here.

'Hey, you look beautiful,' he said. 'Can I get you a drink? Or there are some nibbles over here—'

'Damon.' Her voice didn't even sound like her own. It had authority. Confidence. Surety. All the things she'd never had before in her life... before him.

And now, because of them, she was going to lose him. She could see it in the desperate gleam in his eyes, the way his shoulders slumped as she said his name.

He didn't want her to do this any more than she wanted to do it. But because of him, because of all that she'd learned about herself in the time they'd spent together, she had to.

'I bought you something,' he said, desperately. Fishing something out of his pocket, he held it out in the palm of his hand.

Rachel stared at it. A small felt mouse in a

perfectly fitted red jacket holding a carol sheet in front of him.

She loved it. But she didn't take it. Not yet.

'We need to talk,' she said, instead.

'I know.' She heard defeat in his voice as his fist closed around the poor mouse. 'Come on.'

She followed him into the kitchen, aware that there was some sort of commotion drawing attention behind them, but unwilling to take her eyes off Damon for a second to find out what it was. Theo and Celeste, she imagined. And actually, she didn't want to imagine that any more than she had to.

The kitchen, at least, was quiet, cool and drama free. She'd expected they'd stop there, but Damon kept walking, all the way to the back door, which he opened and drew her out into the bitter December night. She shivered as she followed him across the grass to where a small swing seat hung from a tree at the end of the long, narrow garden. Shrugging off his jacket, Damon wrapped it around her shoulders, then motioned for her to sit.

'Tonight's the last night of our festive fling,' he said wistfully as he sat beside her. And for a moment, Rachel felt a spark of hope deep inside her. Then he flashed her a quick smile and added, 'We made the most of it, didn't we?'

*Yes. So much so that I fell head over heels in love with you.*

He was trying to take control of the conversation, talking over the spaces where she would have spoken, the way her family had done all her life. The way *he* never had before.

*He's scared*, she realised. But why? What could he have to be scared of? The worst that could happen was that Celeste would be cross with him for breaking her heart. If he felt nothing for her beyond their fling, what was there to be scared of?

Unless he was scared because he *did* feel something, and he didn't know what to do about it.

Rachel felt that hope flare up again. She just hoped Damon was brave enough to feel it too.

# CHAPTER FOURTEEN

'IN FACT, I was thinking, maybe we could still get together, now and then, if you wanted. Just casually, of course.' Damon was talking for the sake of talking and he knew it. But if he stopped, he knew Rachel was going to ask him for something he didn't know how to give. So he just kept going. 'It seems a shame to give up such great chemistry completely, right?'

*Please, let it be enough. It's all I know how to give you. Please.*

He just needed time. He wasn't an idiot. He'd known long before Celeste brought it to his attention that he was in over his head here. That what he felt for Rachel wasn't like anything he'd felt before. That was why it was so terrifying.

Hell, he'd known nine years ago that if he got too close to this woman he'd fall. At eighteen he'd been smart enough to run the other way.

Apparently, growing up had made him stupid.

He needed time to figure out what it meant. How it fitted in with who he was. How he could still be *him*, when he felt this way about her.

'I think a spring fling has a nice sound to it

anyway, don't you?' He flashed his best, most charming smile, and hoped.

But Rachel wasn't smiling. He knew that, even in the pitch dark of the winter night, with only faint lights from the windows, the moon and the street lights behind them to help him figure it out.

He stopped talking. People had been talking over Rachel, talking *for* her, for too many years already. He might be a complete arse but he wasn't going to be another of *those* people.

However hard it was, he needed to listen to what she had to say.

'Damon. That's what I came here tonight to tell you. I don't want a fling, festive, spring or otherwise, with you.' She paused, taking a breath, and Damon resisted the urge to interrupt her. Just. 'I'm in love with you. I know that wasn't the deal we made, and it definitely wasn't what I planned but… I knew it was a risk. I've, well, had a crush on you basically the whole time I've known you. I knew I should stay away to protect my own heart, I knew that you didn't do commitment, that you weren't offering anything beyond this Christmas. But the way I feel when I'm with you… Damon, you make me feel like I can do anything, and I want more of that feeling.'

'You *can* do anything,' he told her, because it might be his last chance. 'You're amazing.'

'That's what made me believe I could do this.'

She met his gaze with her own, and even in the half-light he could see the steely determination in it. 'You taught me to ask for what I wanted. So I'm asking. I want *you*, Damon. Not for a fling, or for a season. Forever. I want you to love me the way I love you. I want us to be together. And I think deep down you might want the same thing too. So I'm asking…do you?'

It was as if his world had frozen.

So many years, so many people, jobs, opportunities, and nobody had ever asked him to stay, to commit. Not outright like that. Oh, people had hinted, made suggestions, always couched in terms that allowed them to save face if he said no. And he had always said no, because that wasn't who he was.

For the first time, the smallest corner of his heart wanted to say yes.

But he couldn't.

So he tried to negotiate.

'I'm not ready to say goodbye to you yet, if that's what you mean. So maybe we could—'

'It's not what I mean,' she interrupted him, proving once and for all that she wasn't the shy, easily intimidated Rachel everyone else seemed to think she was. 'I'm not asking you to propose marriage here and now or anything, but I need to know if you're willing to give a relationship between us a proper shot. To admit that this isn't just "colleagues who have sex" or even a festive fling. That what we have *matters*. It's special, and it means something, and you're willing to commit to finding out where that leads us. If you can't do that—'

'I don't commit,' he said, automatically. 'You know that.'

Was it the moonlight that made her expression look so pitying? He hoped so.

'Because you have to keep your options open, right?' She nodded and got to her feet, shrugging off his jacket and laying it on her empty seat. 'Okay, then. Well, in that case, thank you for my first festive fling. It honestly changed my life. I'll see you at work next week.' And with that, she turned her back on him and walked away, taking that part of his heart he'd been ignoring for so long with her.

'Wait!' he called, but while her footsteps slowed, just for a moment, when he couldn't find any more words to follow up with, she didn't stop.

She left him sitting there in his parents' garden, feeling like the biggest idiot known to man.

A feeling that didn't dissipate when his sister appeared a few minutes later, and sat down beside him on the swing, crushing his jacket.

'You are the biggest idiot known to man,' she said.

'I know.' But what else could he have done? Rachel was asking for something he wasn't able to give. Saying no now was far easier on everyone than going along with what she wanted, only to break her heart later when she realised he wasn't the man she'd hoped he could be.

'Let me guess.' Celeste kicked off the floor with one foot, making the old swing seat sway forward and back. 'She asked you to commit and you said no.'

'Basically.'

'Why? Because you wanted to be free to sleep with as many other women as possible?'

'No!' He was pretty sure he'd never find another woman like Rachel anyway. 'Because I'm not that guy. I'd let her down, in the end, when she realised that.'

He needed to keep moving, keep things interesting, seek out new variety in his life. He couldn't afford to become as tunnel-visioned as his parents had always been. He couldn't pass up all the other opportunities that might come his way. Not other women, other relationships. Those were the last things on his mind right now. But committing, settling down, that meant saying no to other things, didn't it? Meant always asking permission, always consulting someone else...

The way his parents never had.

They'd single-mindedly pursued their own interests and expected their children to be interested in the same things. He'd spent his whole life knowing he wasn't good enough for them because he didn't have that same passion for one subject. They'd chosen what mattered to them and gone after it, while he'd tried to take a different path by seeking variety in all things.

In fact, he'd chased constant change the way they'd chased their careers, to the point of ignoring all other options…

He'd thought he was so different from them, but what if he was just making the same mistakes in his own way? What if he'd been so fixated on moving forward that he failed to recognise the one thing worth standing still for?

Love.

'Damon?' Celeste actually sounded concerned, which meant he must look worse than he felt.

'I'm okay.' A lie, but then, she'd know that too.

'For what it's worth? I don't think you'd let her down, little brother.' Standing up, she pressed a quick kiss to his hair, something he couldn't remember her doing since he was a child. 'In fact, I think you've got a better handle on this love thing than most of us. You just need to be brave enough to go after it.'

*Go after it. Go after her.*

As he watched his sister walk away, the same way her best friend had not so long ago, the pieces started to fall into place in Damon's head.

And suddenly, he knew what he had to do.

\* \* \*

Rachel was not going to cry. She was absolutely not crying. She was not—

'Need a tissue back there, love?' The taxi driver reached back between the front seats and handed her one anyway, which was just as well, as she couldn't really talk much through her sobs.

'Christmas can be tough,' he added sagely as she blew her nose. 'Now, let's get you where you need to be.'

Theo had put her in the cab, bless him, and when the driver had asked her where she wanted to go she'd only hesitated for a moment.

She couldn't go home, not knowing that Hannah, Gretchen, Maisie and her dad would be there, playing happy Christmas Eve family. Not when her stepsisters would know instantly what had happened—and wouldn't hesitate to tell her that they had told her so. She needed a little time to herself before that happened.

She'd thought briefly of the department store. It would be empty, she had a key, and she could hide out in her little cupboard office until she felt ready to face the world again.

Except that was going backwards, back to who she had been before. And she wasn't going to do that.

In fact, she'd sent her resignation letter to Hannah by email before heading to the party, just to ensure that she couldn't.

So, with her past behind her, and the future she'd hoped for out of reach, that meant there was only one thing to do.

Build a new future.

'Cressingham Arcade,' she'd said. 'Take me to the arcade.'

Because while the arcade would always be intrinsically linked to Damon in her mind and in her heart, it was also the place where she'd found her professional courage. It was where she'd realised for the first time that her window displays were something people valued, rather than something she was allowed to do as a favour from her stepmother. Where, working with the shopkeepers, she'd finally been able to put into practice all she'd learned in her years of studying, to bring to life all the ideas she had for bringing local businesses to the public eye. She'd been able to help people because she had skills and knowledge they didn't. Ones they valued.

She'd never felt that way before. And she wasn't going to give it up just because Damon wasn't brave enough to face up to what he felt.

Besides, there was one last window she still hadn't managed to transform. And she wanted it done before Christmas morning.

The arcade was in darkness, of course, but as she

let herself in she realised it wasn't actually empty. At the far end of the passageway there was a light on inside one shop. The shop she'd come to visit.

'Mr Jenkins?' Rachel leaned against the open doorway and looked in at the older man sitting hunched over at his desk.

He looked up, apparently unsurprised to see her. 'You're here to finish that window display, I suppose.'

'If you don't mind.'

Mr Jenkins waved a hand towards the window. 'What do I care? It's only my shop.'

That, Rachel decided, was practically an excited request for help, coming from Mr Jenkins.

'I'll get to work, then.'

The display had been building in her imagination for weeks, ever since she'd first visited the shop. Working under Mr Jenkins's watchful eye—for all that he pretended he was paying her no attention at all—she quickly brought together all the elements she'd dreamt of.

There were her mice, of course—those featured in every window, in one way or another. And elements from the other shops in the arcade too, like silk flowers from the florist's, a lace veil from the bridal boutique, beautiful papers and pens from the stationer's, all to display Mr Jenkins's jewels on. But most of the display elements came from the jeweller's itself—not just the rings and necklaces and gems, but the vintage typewriter he kept behind the desk, and the black and white photo of a beautiful young woman from the shelf above it.

'My late wife,' he said, gruffly, when she asked if she could use it. 'She always liked putting on a show. Reckon she'd like to be in your window too.'

It was more than an hour later that she finally stepped outside the shop, stretched out the kinks in her back and neck, and stood back to admire her handiwork.

There, sprawling from left to right across the window display, was the story she wanted to tell. A love story, of course. One that spanned years and continents—courtesy of the vintage clocks and map Mr Jenkins had squirrelled away in a cupboard. One written in piles of letters—delivered by mice, naturally—and culminating in a stunning engagement ring.

Suddenly, one last mouse appeared. A mouse in a red jacket, singing Christmas carols, placed next to the ring by a hand she recognised, although the face attached to it was hidden by the shadows of the shop.

*He must have come in the back way*, her mind noted absently. *Mr Jenkins hates it when he does that.*

But the thought was so surreal, she couldn't quite process it, let alone begin to hope. Maybe she was imagining things. That made more sense than the alternative right now, given the way the rest of the evening had gone.

Rachel stared at the mouse as the hand pulled away, even as she heard the shop door open, and someone join her outside.

'It's perfect.'

At the sound of Damon's voice, the spell broke, and she spun around, the display forgotten.

'What are you doing here?' Anger rose up in her, unexpected and unbidden. This was her future she was chasing. Couldn't he give her one night to move on from their fling?

But Damon shifted his weight from one foot to the other, his expression nervous in the faded yellow of the arcade's vintage lighting.

'I'm here to follow your lead,' he said. 'To finally admit what I want...and ask for it.'

Anger faded. Instead, that flicker of hope, the one she'd swallowed down and tried to ignore as she'd walked away from him, returned. 'And what do you want?' She kept her tone neutral, free from emotion or influence. He needed to tell her, this time. To ask for what he wanted. What they both needed.

'You. If you'll have me.'

'Why?' She hoped his reasons were good. Because it was taking everything she had not to jump into his arms right now.

'Because…because I realised I've been trying so hard not to be my parents I turned into them anyway. Because I never thought I could matter to someone the way I want to matter to you. Because when I'm with you, I don't feel like my worth is weighed out in my achievements or my focus. Because…' He paused, and motioned to the window behind her, turning her around to look at it herself. 'Because I see these perfect worlds you create and I want to make them real for you. I want to give you everything you ask for, everything you can imagine.'

Rachel didn't look away from the window, from the story she'd told there, knowing that the minute she met his gaze again she'd be in his arms. She needed answers first. 'But…you told me no. You said you couldn't. What changed?'

'The world,' he said simply. 'It's so much emptier without you in it.'

'Good answer,' she muttered. 'So, what exactly are you asking for? Another fling?'

She held her breath until she saw him shake his head in the glass of the window. And then, to her astonishment, she saw his reflection drop down to one knee.

Rachel spun around to face him. 'No.'

'Yes,' he said, with a grin. 'I hope.'

'You hate commitment. You hate being tied down to *anything*. Why would you propose to me?'

Damon took her hands in his and tugged her closer. 'Because you don't tie me down. You make me feel like I can take on the world. So, Rachel Charles, will you do me the incredible honour of being my wife?'

It was crazy. She knew it was crazy.

But at the same time…it felt completely right.

She wanted this.

'I'm a little surprised you're not making me ask you,' she joked.

'Feel free.'

Laughing, Rachel dropped to her knees in front of him, mirroring his pose. 'Damon Hunter, will you marry me?'

'In a heartbeat,' he said, and kissed her.

She could feel a lifetime in that kiss. A whole story waiting to be written. She never wanted it to end.

Then Mr Jenkins coughed loudly behind her. 'Suppose you two had better come in and pick a ring, then.'

Rachel met Damon's gaze and found everything she was looking for there. This wasn't a dream.

This was her, awake to her own life at last. To all the possibilities that might give her.

Give *them*. Together.

'Come on,' Damon said. 'You get to choose the ring.'

'Damn right I do,' Rachel replied. 'And then we can go and tell Celeste she gets to be maid of honour. And she's not allowed to wear black.'

Because if she was starting her new life, there was no one else she wanted beside her than the man she loved and her best friend.

She just hoped that one day Celeste would find the kind of forever love that she had. And that when she did, she'd be brave enough to ask for love in return.

\* \* \* \* \*

*Look out for the next story in the
Cinderellas in the Spotlight duet
Coming soon!*

*And if you enjoyed this story,
check out these other great reads from
Sophie Pembroke*

Italian Escape with Her Fake Fiancé
Second Chance for the Single Mom
Snowbound with the Heir
Pregnant on the Earl's Doorstep

*All available now!*